Passage to Zarahemla

A NOVEL

CHRIS HEIMERDINGER

HEIMERDINGER ENTERTAINMENT, INC.

D1005405

OTHER BOOKS AND AUDIO BOOKS BY CHRIS HEIMERDINGER

The Tennis Shoes Adventure Series:

Tennis Shoes Among the Nephites

Gadiantons and the Silver Sword

The Feathered Serpent, Part 1

The Feathered Serpent, Part 2

The Sacred Quest

The Lost Scrolls

The Golden Crown

Warriors of Cumorah

Tower of Thunder

OTHER TITLES:

Eddie Fantastic
(currently out of print, only available at
www.cheimerdinger.com. Soon to be re-released)

Daniel and Nephi

Ben Franklin and the Chamber of Time

A Return to Christmas
(Softcover edition, Ballantine Books. Hardcover edition only available at
www.cheimerdinger.com)

A Light in the Storm
(currently out of print, only available at *www.cheimerdinger.com*)

MOVIES BY CHRIS HEIMERDINGER

Lehi's Land of First Inheritance
(documentary, writer/director)

ISBN 0-97083-430-6

Printed in Canada
10   9   8   7   6   5   4   3   2   1

For Liahona,

I dreamed of you,
I knew you were coming,
and now you're here.
Welcome to the world!

CHAPTER

1

THE HUNTER SQUEEZED THE trigger of his
Winchester 30–06. The blast shattered the dawn and
stirred the mist in the sleepy morning meadow. The
kick of the rifle against his shoulder unleashed a warm rush
of adrenaline.

He lowered the rifle scope from his line of vision, tipped
up the rim of his *No Fear* sports cap, and focused on the
object of his aim—a majestic southern Utah mule deer. For a
moment he held his breath and watched. If his bullet had
missed, the deer surely would have bolted. But the deer did
not bolt. After raising its neck, it held still for two inter-
minable seconds. And then, at last, it staggered and collapsed.

All at once the Hunter's heart dropped. He focused on
the rack of antlers and realized what he had done. But had
he realized it even before he fired his rifle? He truly wasn't
sure.

The Hunter turned as he heard the whoop of his two companions, Clacker and Beaumont, who came up behind him,

running excitedly through the woods. They hadn't seen him pull the trigger, but they could plainly see the russet-colored mound of hide fifty yards distant, partly obscured by mist.

"Swwweet!" said Beaumont, his voice squealing. He was in his late twenties, but his voice still had the strain of a boy of thirteen.

Clacker and Beaumont ran past in earnest, but the Hunter hesitated. Finally he walked forward, the dew from the meadow grass saturating his pant leg, soaking through his sock, and chilling the flesh of his shin. He arrived to find his companions kneeling circumspectly over the deer like detectives at a murder scene. They were no longer whooping. The Hunter let out a long, weary sigh.

Beaumont glanced up at him, one of his molars black with chewing tobacco. "Did you see the rack?"

The Hunter half shrugged, half shook his head.

"Your license is for a doe, right?" asked Clacker.

He nodded.

Clacker huffed, "Musta thought it was your ex-wife in those sights!" The heavyset man snorted with laughter, like a turkey gobble.

The Hunter bristled slightly and sent him a look that transformed the laughter into a clearing of the throat.

Beaumont whistled as he admired the rack. Six-point. Impressive by any standards, especially here in Southern Utah where deer were somewhat smaller than their cousins farther north. He cursed, shaking his crop of bright red hair in disappointment. "That's a cryin' shame, is what *that* is!"

The Hunter leaned forward to see the place where the bullet had entered the animal's ribs. The hole was small. Very little blood. If it was any consolation, it appeared that the deer hadn't suffered much pain. "Well," he began, "let's back up the truck and haul it out of—"

Clacker interrupted, saying bluntly, "You don't wanna do that."

"We can't just leave it," the Hunter protested.

"Sure we can," said Beaumont, rising to his feet. He grabbed a tuft of weeds and tossed it casually over the carcass. "We just cover it over with brush, then—"

Unexpectedly, the deer's legs kicked. Animation electrified its silent body. The men let out exclamations of surprise, hurriedly backing away as the buck rose up onto all four hooves.

"Careful!" Beaumont squealed, almost as if the animal might seek revenge, try to skewer them with its antler tips. But it only scampered out of their midst, fleeing into the brush at the meadow's edge.

Clacker, who'd fallen onto his hind end in the fracas, was laughing hysterically. The Hunter, however, was not laughing. He looked frantically for the deer in his rifle scope, finding only a blizzard of branches and brambles, underbrush and leaves, much of it yellowing with the advent of winter. The deer had disappeared.

"Problem solved!" Clacker announced, clapping his hands in triumph.

The Hunter gritted his teeth and started jogging across the meadow.

"What are you doin'?" asked Beaumont.

"It's gonna die sooner or later," the Hunter called back. "I don't want it to suffer." He continued into the underbrush.

"Let it go!" Clacker called after him.

Clacker's laughter was contagious, and Beaumont finally succumbed. They watched the Hunter vanish into the tangle of scrub oak, elm, and black willow.

"We're not waiting!" Clacker cried, though already the Hunter was almost out of hearing.

The Hunter turned once to confirm that his companions weren't following, then faced forward again in disgust. He forged deeper into the woods, eyes peeled for any sign of blood or other evidence that would reveal his quarry's trail.

He found a track along the path and a tuft of hide on a broken branch, confirming that he was at least headed in the right direction.

Soon he arrived at a pond that he remembered from his childhood. The place hadn't changed. The trunks and other deadfall that stuck up out of the water were bleached white by the years, reminding him of images and photographs he'd seen of mass graves filled with old and rotting skeletons. Carefully, he walked around its steep edges, circumventing a rather nasty patch of briars. But as he walked across the muddy bank on the opposite side, he stopped suddenly. He felt something strange, but—

The ground began to vibrate. *An earthquake!* The Hunter caught himself as he was thrown off balance; his breath snagged in his throat. The leaves were rustling all around him, many breaking free and floating to the ground. The surface of the pond was agitated, like a kettle on the boil.

But two seconds later, it ended. The ground beneath his feet became stable. He looked at the pond. Tiny waves lapped against the shore. One of the whitewashed trunks out in the middle of the water slowly toppled over, creating a small splash.

His mind continued to reel in astonishment. Not an earthquake, he concluded. A tremor. Nevertheless, it had been a long time since he'd felt anything this strong, not since the first year after he moved to California. The Hunter hesitated another moment. Then, at last, he moved on into the deeper woods.

However, after searching a while longer, he began to feel quite peculiar—even uneasy. Something was different. He couldn't put his finger on it. It was as if . . . he didn't know this place anymore. Didn't recognize the patch of trees on his left, or the taller trees ahead. Odd. He'd have sworn that he knew every inch of this country. He used to explore here every day of his life. Just ahead he heard the trickle of a stream. The sound was reassuring. If he heard a stream, he knew he was very near the middle of the hollow.

The woods he'd entered were bizarre, spectral-looking, like something gothic or ancient. This hollow had seen many flash floods over the centuries. As a result, the trees were mangled and twisted, growing out of the earth at odd, contorted angles. There were as many dead trunks as living ones, but the living trees tangled themselves around the dead, as if drawing them into the living fold. Or perhaps it was the other way around—the dead trees were trying to suffocate the living. One could imagine any shape, any pattern, if he studied the misty woods long enough: vengeful ghosts and long-fingered sorcerers, brooding phantoms and tortured corpses.

The Hunter had heard many stories about this country, and these woods in particular. Tales of weird noises and optical illusions. The Hunter had never experienced any of that, but the stories had never entirely faded from his mind. Some locals believed the hollow was haunted. But such was the tendency, he decided, of any folks who liked to think their plot of earth was more interesting than it actually was.

All at once, he caught a glimpse of russet-colored fur dashing through the undergrowth. But then it vanished again into a section of woods that was particularly dark and dense. The Hunter grumbled in frustration. Why wouldn't it just *die?* Still, he admired its tenacity—its will to survive. Weariness was settling over him. His thirst was mounting. Maybe his companions were right. Maybe it *was* better to let it go. What if the wound wasn't fatal? What if the bullet had gone completely through without damaging any organs? He scoffed at himself. He'd *seen* the wound. He saw where it had entered the creature's torso. The buck was going to die. It was just a matter of time.

He forced his way through a tight knot of branches, leaving scratches on his face. The gurgle of the stream increased in volume. This heartened him, and he licked his lips. The water was beckoning.

But then he paused. A new and even more unusual feeling coiled up inside him. He swore he heard a breeze, yet nothing stirred. Mist continued to blur the background thirty feet in any direction. A somber whistling began to rise in volume, like a teapot at the end of a long, hollow tunnel. Seconds later the whirring faded, but what replaced it was more curious yet—and chilling. There were whispers in the woods. Faint and garbled, as if the forest were exchanging secrets. For an instant it almost sounded like the chant of a séance, faraway and echoing. His eyes peered into the depths of the foliage, searching for anything that might be moving.

He turned quickly and looked behind him, but it was impossible to pinpoint a source for the noise. Branches crisscrossed around him like barbwire barricades. Shafts of sunlight cut sharply through the autumn canopies like lights emitting from the long fingertips of holy angels. Or unholy demons. The feeling around him certainly wasn't hallowed. A shiver ran from his tailbone to the back of his neck.

"Hello?" he said into the mist, his tone slightly breathless.

Somehow his voice had a hushing effect. The whispers ceased. Or moved away. His eyes tried to follow them, but failed. The Hunter swallowed heavily, his heart now hammering like a drum.

"Beaumont? Clacker?"

Again, there was no reply. Nor could he hear more wind or whispers. The Hunter removed his cap and used his sleeve to wipe the sweat from his brow.

He tried once more to shake off the creepiness, and then he continued on, pushing past a series of branches with still-green leaves. At last he saw the stream. A crisp column of light illuminated the water like a current of jewels. His eyes followed it a few yards upstream, beneath the brooding branches of a massive oak, where there was a place to kneel and drink.

After pulling his legs through the last tangle of branches, he stumbled into the open space. His mouth felt as dry as charcoal. Again he studied the forest, his mind stirring with anxiety. Except for the stream, the woods were silent. The water at his feet flowed as clear as glass. Nevertheless, he waited another long moment, feeling vulnerable and wary, like any other animal before it knelt to drink.

But why was he so frightened? There were no whispers now. No wind. He'd foolishly allowed his imagination to get away from him. He *knew* this place. Undoubtedly he'd passed by this very spot many times. He wanted to laugh at himself, but couldn't. Something internal suggested it was the sound of his voice, the pattern of his breaths, that had brought on the last episode of noises. He realized his quest to find the deer had come to an end. He only wanted to get out of these woods.

He got down on one knee, and then the other. After setting his rifle on the lichen-covered stones, he dipped his hands in the cool current. As soon as he'd washed the dirt from his palms, he splashed some of the water on his face. The feeling revived him, *sobered* him. Carefully, he cupped both hands into the spring, his fingers attempting to filter any impurities stirred up by the current. Then he proceeded to draw the water toward his mouth.

But before the drink arrived, his hands stopped. Something splashed into his palms, mingling with the pure water and forming a gauzy pink cloud. His eyes widened. The air was sucked from his lungs like a vacuum. *Blood!* It had fallen from above!

After another drip turned the water in his hands an awful red, he flung it away, as if tossing poison or excrement. Dread filled his mind, swirling like a cyclone. He tilted his neck, focusing upward into the branches. A new droplet splattered on his cheek; another hit the blue fabric of his *No Fear* sports cap.

The Hunter scrambled backwards, his face contorted with shock. A pair of black, lifeless eyes were staring down at him. The source of blood was a long snout with dark nostrils.

It was the *deer! His* deer! He recognized the place in its ribs where his bullet had entered. The carcass hung over a branch four feet overhead. The legs were tethered by a crude-looking rope. Several gaping slashes stretched along its length, as if someone had begun the process of skinning its hide. There was an arrow in its neck. An *arrow!*

The Hunter hyperventilated; the questions were flying faster than his mind could grasp them. His fear became primeval, shooting through his veins like cold explosions. But then his attention was wrenched a different direction.

The whispering returned, louder, more distorted and angry. And with the whispers came shadows. The forest in all directions was *crawling* with shadows. Not bodies—not living souls—but indistinguishable wraiths with bloody, blackened faces and piercing white eyes. The whole forest had become a vortex of chaos and aggression.

An echoing twang rang out at his right. Simultaneously, his shoulder felt a nerve-shattering pain. His body twisted around, crashing into the trunk of the oak tree. The *No Fear* hat fell off his head. He collapsed to his knees. He'd been *shot!* His focus fell on the shaft of an arrow, protruding from his right shoulder. The feathers were blue and exotic, the wood banded by colorful designs, like something from another age. He reached back and felt the arrowhead sticking out behind his shoulder, so sharp it cut his finger. Panic avalanched through his soul. The whispers had escalated to screeching, like a swarm of ravens. The shadows from the woods were descending on him like wolves. His uninjured arm flew up to shield his face.

The Hunter screamed.

2

KERRA MCCONNELL WATCHED solemnly as the morticians and cemetery workers lowered her mother's casket into the earth. Her eleven-year-old brother, Brock, stood beside her, frowning a bit, but otherwise it was an expression that she couldn't discern. The casket was cheap—pine with a lacquer finish, the cheapest on the price list. Such was the going rate for funerals paid for by the State of California.

Just across the rectangular grave that had been dug into the earth stood their social worker, Mr. Paulson. He was a mousy-looking man in thick, silver glasses. On his head was a dark crop of black hair that he'd tried to comb over a conspicuous bald patch. Kerra didn't like him much. What was worse, she didn't *trust* him. Her life was in his hands, as well as the life of her brother. The concept made Kerra shudder. Yes, they were orphans now. But somewhere in this universe there had to be a better plan than this—placing the fate of two people in the hands of a man who smelled perpetually of body odor mingled with Old Spice aftershave.

Four days earlier her mother had died from an overdose. The event wasn't really a surprise to Kerra or her brother. Delia McConnell had been a heavy drug user, smoker, and drinker for as long as they could remember. Seventeen-year-old Sakerra had done all that she could to help her—as much help as a teenager could give in such circumstances. But in the end, Kerra's efforts had proved futile. Now she and Brock were alone in a world that was trying desperately to tear them apart.

Kerra realized now that all they had left was each other. Of course, in many ways, this was all that they had *ever* had. Their father had abandoned them early on. Kerra had been only five years old at the time. Their mother had made a meager effort to raise them, but for the most part Kerra had been the acting mother in their family. She'd taken care of Brock, taken care of Delia, and, to the best of her abilities, taken care of herself.

Despite it all, Kerra McConnell had grown into a remarkably beautiful young woman, though this was not the image that she saw in the mirror. She really didn't spend much time in front of such things. Her long, blonde hair hung lazily, almost poetically, around her shoulders. Her eyes were a sweltering blue sea, full of passion and determination, though of late that passion was only for one thing: to survive. In other circumstances—"normal" circumstances—Kerra might have been a cheerleader, a class president, or a prom queen. But she had no such aspirations. By necessity, she was already an adult by the time she was five. Things that other seventeen-year-old girls considered matters of life and death, Kerra saw as frivolous and weak. After all, she'd always had her mother to take care of, and her brother's soul to save.

Brock was, in the words of some at the office of Welfare and Family Services, a typical product of his environment— angry, rebellious, and antisocial. Most felt his chances in life were slim. What was worse, Brock knew what they thought of him. He didn't have to hear them say it; he sensed it instinctively. However, he also had a nasty habit of eavesdropping. Because no one had much hope for him, he honestly didn't have much hope for himself. As with Kerra, his life's passions were dedicated to survival. But *unlike* Kerra, he'd adopted his own methods to achieve this. He would gladly take and scrounge and manipulate whenever he could—wherever the opportunity presented itself. Strangely, only his sister seemed to view him as anything but a parasite, a waif, or a future Public Enemy Number One. But what did she know?

Lately the two of them had had many clashes over curfews and rules and other stuff that Brock felt were none of his sister's business. He much preferred the company of Spree and the other members of the Shamans—the local street gang who hung out at the Stonewood Mall and the back alleys of Downey, California.

In January he was arrested for hot-wiring a '61 Lincoln Continental convertible. On that occasion his older accomplice had taken most of the rap, yet it was Brock who'd successfully crossed the wires and driven the car from the scene. His mother, always able to play the role of the overwrought single parent for onlookers, had convinced the authorities it would never happen again. But the police now had their eye on young Brock McConnell. As it happened, it was Kerra who'd actually enforced any discipline, enacting curfews, installing locks on his bedroom window to keep him inside at night, and chasing him down whenever he slipped past security. That was just before their mother began her final descent into the abyss.

For the children's sake, the mortician gave a kind of graveside memorial, which took all of three and a half minutes. Kerra looked up at the sky. The day was particularly bright and sunny, a fact that vexed her soul. Funerals were supposed to take place in the rain, right? Black umbrellas, huddled masses, the smell of wet streets and musty tombs. Instead, it was a perfect day for the beach, and the irony offended her. This was the blackest day of her life—a day she'd been dreading for years, a day she'd desperately hoped might not arrive until she was old enough to become Brock's legal guardian.

As they walked across the cemetery's manicured lawn toward the social worker's car, Mr. Paulson said the obligatory, "I'm sorry about your mother."

He tried to sound sincere. He really did. But to Kerra it just sounded routine. All in a day's work for a California social worker.

Brock spoke his first words of the afternoon as they climbed into the '91 Pontiac Sunbird. "I don't see why we had to go to this dumb thing anyway."

As Kerra sat beside him in the backseat she tried to take his hand, but he pulled it away.

An hour later, they were in Mr. Paulson's office. Also present were a man and woman whom Kerra didn't recognize. Nevertheless, she realized why they were here. And the realization made her heart feel like it was being squeezed in a mop strainer. The couple were obviously state-compensated foster parents. She and Brock had been told they were coming, but somehow it didn't seem real. Nothing about these past four days had seemed real.

"Unfortunately," Mr. Paulson began, "we can't keep you together. In a situation like this where the father is gone and there are no known relatives . . ." He looked up thoughtfully and asked the same question he'd already asked twice before. "Are you sure you have no idea where your father might . . . ?"

Kerra shook her head impatiently. "No. He left us. Brock doesn't even remember him."

Mr. Paulson sighed and sat back in his seat. "As you

know, in this kind of situation our options are rather limited. Mr. and Mrs. Fleagle have agreed to take Brock. For you, Kerra, we'll soon have—"

"We won't be separated," said Kerra bluntly.

Mr. Paulson sighed and removed his spectacles, a gesture apparently meant to show compassion, though it seemed rehearsed. "I know how you feel—"

"No," said Kerra. "You don't." She put her arm around Brock and drew him closer. "We won't be separated."

Mrs. Fleagle, an austere-looking woman with crooked teeth, looked from Mr. Paulson to Kerra and back to Mr. Paulson. "I-I'm afraid we don't have room for a boy *and* a girl—"

"We don't need anyone else," Kerra insisted. "I can take care of him. I've *been* taking care of him."

"I'm sorry, Kerra," said Mr. Paulson tiredly. "The law is quite clear. You're only seventeen. And where the boy already has a criminal record—"

"We'll move," she replied curtly. "I'll get a job. We'll be all right."

Her voice had an edge of desperation. Brock studied the patterns in the floor tile, doing his best to slouch and look unconcerned. But Kerra wasn't fooled. The boy was scared to death.

Mr. Paulson shook his head. "It's out of the question. Maybe in the future we can make more permanent arrangements where you're both in the same household."

"Can you guarantee that?" asked Kerra.

Mr. Paulson hesitated. It was a fatal hesitation, and Kerra sensed it. Nevertheless, the caseworker replied, "We'll do everything that we can."

At that moment Kerra made her decision. But she had to play the game. She had to buy a little more time.

"All right," she said, her voice full of defeat. "But he's not even packed. All of our things are still at the apartment. Let me help him pack tonight. Mr. and Mrs. Fleagle can pick him up there in the morning."

Mr. Fleagle mumbled something about having very little room for more suitcases, considering that they were already caring for three other foster children. Kerra assured him that Brock's things wouldn't take up much space. Mr. Paulson finally blew a sigh and consented. He even agreed to drive them home.

"But just to gather your things," he hastily added. "You'll both sleep at the center tonight." He turned to the Fleagles. "Brock should be ready around eight A.M."

An hour later, as the summer sun sank into the Pacific, they arrived at their apartment complex on Stimson Street. Mr. Paulson had grown increasingly nervous the whole way there. Kerra might have thought he'd seen plenty of neighborhoods with residents who were primarily Hispanic, black, or from other minorities, but what she didn't know was that Carson Paulson had made it a point throughout his career to work out of an office and not in the field. As they pulled into the parking lot, several tattoo-spangled bystanders eyed them suspiciously.

"Is it safe to park my car here?" Mr. Paulson asked the children.

Facetiously, Brock replied, "Yeah, I'd be worried. Old Pontiacs are in high demand."

"This may take us a couple hours," said Kerra. "We can meet you back here when we're finished."

Mr. Paulson glanced around again at the run-down neighborhood and the tattoos.

"They don't like strangers much," Brock informed him.

Mr. Paulson looked at his watch. "All right. But I'll only give you *one* hour. Be ready."

Kerra and Brock climbed out of the backseat. They watched as Mr. Paulson drove away. As soon as he was out of sight, Kerra grabbed her brother's arm and hoisted him toward the apartment.

"C'mon," she said.

"Huh?" said Brock, confused.

"Don't act so surprised. We're getting out of here."

•   •   •

Brock waited until they were inside the apartment, pulling duffel bags and their mother's lone travel trunk out of the closet, before he asked the obvious.

"Where are we going?"

"Does it matter?" said Kerra. "We're staying together."

"What if I don't *want* to go?" said Brock. "All my friends are here."

Kerra turned to her brother, her emotions torn between sympathy and frustration. "Don't you get it? In a foster home you won't see them anyway. We won't see each other either. Do you want them to separate us forever?"

He thought a moment, then confessed, "No."

"Do you want them to make it so we can't ever be together again?"

Her words simmered in the boy's mind. At last he shook his head and remarked, "I hate them."

Kerra shuffled through the drawer next to the fridge until she found keys to her mother's '94 Ford Taurus. Delia McConnell still owed three thousand on the car, which was far more than it was presently worth. Despite this, no payments had been made for several months. Taped to the fridge was a threat to repossess it, but as of four days ago the threat had yet to be carried out. Kerra pressed the duffel bag into Brock's arms.

"Fill it," she ordered him.

Brock shuffled down the hallway to his bedroom. He continued to listen to his sister ranting about how they

15

would be forced to live on opposite sides of the world, how nobody really cared, and how they had to look out for each other because "no one else would." She also mentioned that they had only eighty-six dollars to their name.

For Brock it was all just too much to take in. And yet there was no denying a certain element of *adventure* to it all. Just him and Kerra against the world. Then again, hadn't it always been like that? Brock shivered. He wasn't quite sure why. Was it really the thought of losing his sister forever? This was actually a strange revelation. Until today he'd always considered her a major pain in the neck.

As Brock entered his room, he stopped unexpectedly. *How strange.* His bedroom window was sitting open. What was more, it was still swinging slightly—and there was no wind. Then he saw the padlock that his sister had installed on the outside. The loop had been snipped.

Suddenly a hand seized Brock's face, pressing hard against his mouth. He tried to shriek, but the sound was squelched. Brock turned to see his attacker, and immediately his shoulders relaxed. It was Spree, his eighteen-year-old *compadre* and fellow gang member. He had a finger to his lips, earnestly motioning to Brock not to make a sound. Spree was decked in his usual grunge attire, double earrings in his ears and another stud just below his lip. Around his forehead was the red and black bandanna of their gang, the Shamans.

Spree finally released the boy's mouth.

"What are you *doing* here?" Brock whispered urgently.

"Shhh!" said Spree, peeking out the doorway to make sure Kerra was still off in the kitchen.

Brock was beside himself. "If my sister finds you here, she'll *freak!*"

"Then stop whispering so loud!"

For the first time Brock noticed a small leather gym bag in Spree's left hand. It had a double zipper locked in the

16

middle with a tiny padlock to insure the bag's inaccessibility. Spree moved to the window and peeked out nervously into the night.

"You broke into my room?" Brock asked in surprise.

"Had to." Spree turned back and said solemnly, "Hey, I heard about your old lady. Awful thing. But we all knew it would go down sooner or later. How are you doin'?"

"All right," said Brock, his tone noncommittal.

Despite his condolences, Spree seemed distracted by other things. He was acting downright agitated. Spree was always a bit jumpy, but tonight he was more wound up than Brock had ever seen him.

After checking the hallway one more time, Spree went back to Brock and said, "You and me are brothers, right? Partners?"

"Sure, Spree, but—"

"Then I got a favor to ask." He locked eyes with the boy and announced, "I'm ditchin' the Shamans."

"Ditchin'?"

"Quittin' the gang. I'm out, man. Movin' on. I need you to look after something for a while." Spree brought the bag forward.

"What is it?" asked Brock.

"Never mind. No peeking."

"But we're leaving, Spree."

"Leavin'? Where're ya goin'?"

"I don't know yet. We're leavin' town. Tonight."

Spree thought about this a moment, then declared, "Perfect."

Again he peeked around the bedroom door, still wary of Kerra. Then he grabbed Brock's duffel bag and took the liberty of placing his padlocked leather bag inside it. Spree proceeded to hoist clothing from Brock's dresser drawers, as if burying his property the way a dog might bury a bone.

"You call me at my cousin's when you get to where

17

you're going," Spree continued. He handed the boy a small square card with the number on back.

"But I don't know when that'll be," said Brock.

"Doesn't matter. Just call. How would you feel about going into business together? You and me?"

"Yeah," said Brock uncertainly. "Sure."

Spree grabbed Brock's shoulder to shake some enthusiasm into him. "I knew it! We're a team! How many cars did we spring together? Ten? Fifteen?"

"Three," Brock corrected.

Spree ignored that and indicated the duffel bag and his buried property. "Don't lose it. I'm trusting you. I love ya, kid. I've always loved ya. Together we can do it all!"

"All of *what?*" It was Kerra. Brock's sister was standing right in the bedroom doorway. Spree and Brock looked up, startled. Kerra entered, her eyes shooting flames.

"Hey, Kerra!" said Spree, smooth as snake oil. "Ooo, you look fine. New pants? My, my, my . . ."

"How did you get in here?" Kerra demanded.

"Uh, well—"

Kerra saw the open window, the broken lock. Her tone rose to a fever pitch. "You broke into my house?"

Brock glanced at the duffel bag to confirm that Spree's leather bag was well hidden.

Spree raised his hands innocently. "Just sayin' good-bye to the kid—"

"*Get out!*" raged Kerra. She grabbed up a ratty, warped tennis racket from off Brock's shelf and drew it back threateningly.

"I'm out!" said Spree, moving toward the window. "I'm out!"

"NOW!"

Spree hesitated, grinning crookedly. "Not even a good-bye kiss?"

Kerra stepped toward him and swung. The racket barely missed Spree's nose.

"Kidding!" Spree half climbed, half leaped outside.

Brock ran to the window before his friend had dropped down. "I'll call you."

"No, he won't!" Kerra shouted back at him. "Get outa here, Spree!"

Brock and Spree smacked down on each other's fists—a gesture of camaraderie. "Brothers," said Spree. "Don't forget."

Brock nodded.

Kerra pulled Brock away and struck down onto the windowsill with the racket, hitting Spree's knuckle. Spree dropped the last three feet, landing awkwardly on the hedge. Kerra and Brock's eighty-year-old neighbor, Mrs. Dunquist, poked her nose out of her bedroom window to check out the commotion.

Spree explained to the woman, "Little love spat. You know how it is." He turned back to Kerra. "You'll forgive me, won't ya, honey? Sugar lips?"

"Don't ever talk to my brother again!" Kerra hissed.

Spree backed away, throwing kisses. Brock's window slammed shut. Mrs. Dunquist, frowning in disapproval, also disappeared. Spree laughed one final time, then all at once he went silent, again nervously scanning the dark corners all around him. At last, the young gangster picked up his bolt cutters off the grass, put the other hand in his pocket and slipped hastily into the night.

• • •

"You still haven't said where we're going," Brock said in a low voice.

"Don't worry about it," Kerra replied.

Toting a trunk nearly as large as herself, Kerra led her brother through the parking stalls. Brock was also loaded down, not only with the duffel bag, but with several three-ring binders full of Yu-Gi-Oh and Pokemon collector cards. Like Spree, Brock and Kerra were also wary of the night. Kerra feared this was all too easy. She half expected Mr. Paulson to pop out from behind a car, shining a flashlight in their faces.

As they reached the stall assigned to their apartment number, their hearts dropped to their toes. The stall was empty. Their mother's car was conspicuously absent.

"I *told* you she wasn't making payments," said Brock.

"I knew that already," Kerra snapped back.

Brock added, "The repo dude got himself a Ford Taurus."

The devastation weighed heavily on Kerra. "What are we gonna do?" she mumbled to herself. She had no plan B. *What was their plan B?*

Her brother suddenly yanked her down behind the pickup truck parked in the neighboring stall. They peered over the hood as Mr. Paulson's Sunbird rolled slowly down the main avenue of the parking lot, finally stopping at the curb about twenty-five yards away.

"He's early," Brock whispered.

They could see Mr. Paulson's silhouette behind the wheel, checking his watch, looking anxiously toward the building where their apartment was located.

Kerra looked behind her to ascertain an escape route. She was determined that no matter what she and her brother finally decided to do, it did *not* include allowing themselves to be apprehended again by California Welfare and Family Services.

"Let's go," said Kerra.

Brock was still holding her sleeve. "Wait a minute."

As they watched, Mr. Paulson began climbing out of the car, looking impatient. In his hands was a piece of paper where he'd evidently written Kerra and Brock's apartment number. After nervously scoping the area for thugs or villains, he started toward the stairway of their building.

"Follow me," said Brock.

Kerra watched her brother creep around to the other side of the pickup.

"Where are you going?" she asked.

Brock didn't reply. He continued toward Mr. Paulson's car. Reluctantly, Kerra picked up her trunk and went after him. It was on the tip of her tongue to demand that he come back so they could flee in the other direction, but curiosity had the best of her—at least until her brother reached through a narrow gap in the rear window and unlocked the back door. Kerra seemed to recall that Brock had rolled that window down beforehand, almost as if he'd *planned* this. Or if not planned, *hoped*.

"What are you doing?" Kerra whispered harshly.

Brock hardly paused in his actions. "You wanna get out of here, right?"

After slipping into the backseat of the Pontiac, Brock climbed awkwardly into the front seat and took up a position behind the steering wheel. Kerra watched him disappear, sliding into the foot space underneath. She moved around for a better view and saw him pry off some plastic paneling. He started fumbling with some wires just below the steering column. Kerra glanced around in terror. Mr. Paulson would soon realize they'd left the apartment. Surely he would hastily return to his car. Her heart was hammering.

All at once she heard the Pontiac's engine turn over. The exhaust pipe chugged out a puff of smoke. Her brother had hot-wired their social worker's car! Kerra felt completely torn. She wanted to tear Brock's hair out, and at the same time she wanted to kiss him. Brock, with a smug grin on his face, reached over and unlocked the passenger-side door. He even gave it a push to open it.

"Get in!" he invited.

Kerra hesitated, then finally tossed their luggage into the backseat. Nevertheless, she wasn't *about* to climb into the passenger's seat. Spree and the rest of the Shamans may have successfully taught her brother how to hot-wire a car, but she wasn't about to let him drive. She opened the driver's side door and barked, "Move over!"

Brock did as requested, but his grin was still wide. "Sis, I didn't think you had it in ya," he chuckled.

Kerra rolled down her window for a better view of the stairway and hall where Mr. Paulson had disappeared. She threw the car into gear and gingerly pressed down on the gas.

"Punch it!" said Brock. "Let's make like Zorro and X-it!"

"It's a *parking lot,*" Kerra snapped back. "You want me to kill somebody? Besides, Zorro makes a 'Z,' you nerd."

As they approached the gate of the parking area, Kerra saw something that made her eyes thin. It was a black Acura NSX-T sports car. Usually she saw it with the top down, but tonight the top was up, making it impossible to see the faces of the riders. She could feel the vibration of the rap music emanating from within though, like a pulse from the epicenter of an earthquake. Since her own window was wide open, she was terribly afraid the car's occupants would recognize her. Such fears were confirmed as the car lurched forward, blocking her from driving into the street.

The rap music fell silent. All four doors of the Acura flew open. Out stepped the most notorious members of the Shaman street gang. There were six in all. Leading the way as they approached the Pontiac was Torrence Ventura, or, as everyone called him, "Hitch." He had broad shoulders and the lightless eyes of a shark. He was also the largest of the Shamans, standing at just over six-three. Kerra was sure this was why they'd made him their leader, for in the animal world of Los Angeles gangs size mattered, and might made right. But she also suspected his leadership role had something to do with his ruthlessness. There were awful rumors of the things he'd done, particularly to anyone who showed

22

disloyalty. How, she mourned again, had her brother gotten mixed up with sewer vermin like this?

He'd been the Shamans' illustrious leader for the last two years—ever since a rival gang had gunned down the previous leader in Kimberly Park. Some suspected that Hitch had actually tipped off the other gang as to that Shaman leader's whereabouts. Since then Hitch had transformed the Shamans into a power to be reckoned with. Drugs. Burglary. Carjacking. Whatever paid the bills. And they had powerful support from the most notorious branch of the Russian Mafia in California. But tonight Torrence "Hitch" Ventura had a serious problem.

He swaggered up to Kerra's window while the rest of his henchmen surrounded the Pontiac on all sides. He was wearing the black and gray sports coat that had become his trademark over the top of a tight T-shirt that showed off his pecs. Like Spree, he had plenty of earrings. Any facial hair was reserved for his lower lip, deliberately shaved into a narrow stripe that came to a point at the end of his chin. Around his forehead was the same red and black headband worn by Spree—the same headband worn by every Shaman.

Hitch balanced his arm on Kerra's window.

"Nice ride," he remarked sarcastically, glancing over the Sunbird. "New?"

"Get out of our way, Hitch," Kerra demanded.

Hitch feigned insult. "What are ya trippin' for? I'm just bein' friendly." He looked over at Brock in the passenger's seat. "How's it goin,' kid?"

"Good, Hitch," said Brock in a tone of deference.

Hitch pointed at Brock's forehead. "Where's your bandanna?"

"Packed," Brock replied.

"Those are your colors. You should be wearing 'em proudly."

"Move your funeral wagon, please," said Kerra.

Hitch grabbed his heart. "Ouch! That hurts." He glanced into the backseat. "What's with the luggage? You two goin' on a trip?"

"As long as it's away from you," Kerra replied.

"Hey, I was sorry to hear about your mother," said Hitch, attempting to sound genuine, but failing.

Another young man nodded and added, "Good customer."

He was the shiftiest looking of the bunch. Kerra knew him only as Adder. A knife wound to the face had made one of his eyes lazy. Kerra wondered if the eye was real. It might have been made out of glass. As Adder grinned, Hitch gave him a nasty scowl, as if to say the comment was in terribly poor taste.

But something else was on Hitch's mind. He leaned down so that both of them might hear his next question. "Have you seen Spree?"

Kerra glanced up, momentarily ensnared by the gang leader's determined gaze. She feared that she'd paused too long, but Brock piped up.

"No, Hitch," he said.

Hitch studied them closely. "Sure?"

"Is he missing?" asked Brock innocently.

"You could say that," said Hitch. "I really need to talk to him. I really do."

There was a venomous edge to Hitch's tone. Still, that wasn't Kerra's concern. She loathed this person and everything he stood for. The Shamans had recruited her brother when he was the most vulnerable, promising him loyalty, friendship, and a place where he could feel like he belonged—things Brock certainly craved. But Kerra would rather have seen her brother in a nest of scorpions. The truth was, they were only using him. He had served as a lookout, a delivery boy, and goodness knew what else.

Kerra'd had enough. "Let go of my door, you jerk."

Hitch grinned and leaned further into the car. "Always so unfriendly. Why are you so unfriendly? Such a pretty thing. I could do things for you. You could use someone to watch over you. Protect you. Especially if you're gonna be out so late at night."

He tried to touch her cheek. Kerra brutally swatted the hand away. The other Shamans laughed.

Kerra heard a voice call out behind them.

"HEYYY!"

She could see Mr. Paulson in the rearview mirror, running toward them. Kerra decided she had no other choice, and hit the gas. The Pontiac lurched forward. Hitch and his cronies backed away as she yanked on the steering wheel, attempting to escape through the narrow gap between the curb and the front bumper of Hitch's NSX-T.

"Watch the car!" Hitch growled.

She successfully threaded the gap, half wishing she might have failed, maybe left a nice scratch and dent in the Acura's paint job. But the last thing she needed right now was to provoke the ire of the Shamans and get them chasing her through the streets of Los Angeles. The Pontiac bounced over the corner of the curb and fishtailed into the street.

Hitch called after them as they sped away. "If you see Spree, tell him I'm lookin' for him. Hurry back now!"

Mr. Paulson arrived in the midst of the Shamans, winded and infuriated. "They stole my car!" he raved. "Does anyone have a phone? Can anyone . . . ?"

He looked around at the faces of the gangsters and suddenly realized that having his car stolen may have been the least of his problems. A few were snickering, while others seemed to be circling around him.

"Nice shoes," said Adder. "I really wish I had me a pair of shoes like that."

"I kinda like his pants," said another gangster.

Mr. Paulson swallowed.

25

3

THE CALIFORNIA DESERT was a lonely place, particularly at night. Maybe it was just the view from I-15. Maybe, thought Kerra, beyond those desiccated flats and sunburned mesas were rich, green oases and cool, flowing water. She'd come to learn that interstates could create that sort of illusion. Who would want to build a freeway across the best looking land? You'd build it across the ugliest, harshest-looking country possible so that the landscape remained pure and pristine. Kerra was convinced that only two-lane roads could take you to the world's beautiful places. Two-lane roads or hiking trails.

Today she would seek to find one of those private oases. She'd search for a place that she hadn't seen in a dozen years. Not since she was five or six years old. She would seek it from memory. All she remembered for certain was that it was a very short distance from an ugly, unremarkable interstate.

Brock felt as glum as he could possibly feel. Was his sister serious? Was she really planning never to return? It was all so depressing. If they stayed, they'd be separated—maybe forever. But by leaving, Brock was bidding farewell to the only place on earth that he'd ever known. It was like a horrible video game where any path you choose leads to ultimate destruction.

"Are you gonna tell me now?" Brock asked. He really didn't expect his sister to answer. She'd been dodging the question for the last three hours, probably hoping he'd fall asleep, but Brock had never felt so awake in his life.

She surprised him as she said, "Utah."

"*Utah?*" Brock shot back. "What's in Utah?"

"Relatives."

Brock's eyebrows shot up. "I thought you always said we didn't have any relatives."

"We don't," said Kerra. "Not really. These are relatives from . . . from our dad's side of the family."

Now Brock was truly flabbergasted. "Our *dad's side?*"

"Yes."

"How long since—?"

Kerra didn't wait for him to finish the question. "I haven't seen them since I was five or six years old."

"Are you serious? Then why in the h—!"

"Don't use that language!" Kerra scolded. "We're just gonna visit. It's not permanent. They may even help us."

"Help us *how?* I've never even *heard* of these people. How come we've never gone back so I could meet them?"

"That was Mom's choice. She didn't like them. They're Mormons."

"Huh?"

"You've never heard of Mormons?" Kerra asked.

"Not really. Are they like gypsies or those guys who shave their heads and sit like this?" He demonstrated by crossing his legs on the seat, pressing his palms together in front of his face, and making an *ommmm* sound.

"I don't think so, but they're weird in other ways. Haven't

you ever seen those guys who ride bikes with white shirts and ties when the weather is a hundred degrees?"

"Yeah. I guess so."

"But it gets weirder. Once a month they're not allowed to eat. They don't smoke or drink beer or coffee. And they're always praying."

"You remember all this from when you were five?"

"Vividly."

"What else is weird? Can they eat meat?"

"Probably not. At least not ham or baloney. You also have to take a year's supply of food wherever you go."

"Even to school?"

"No, dumkoff," Kerra replied, rolling her eyes. "To school I think they just have to take a seventy-two-hour survival kit. They believe the end of the world could happen at any time. And don't cuss around them. They believe you'll go straight to hell if you cuss."

"Ouch," said Brock. "Straight?"

"Don't pass go, don't collect two hundred dollars. Mom used to say they got more ways of going to hell than anybody on earth."

"Sounds like a fun family," said Brock sarcastically, lacking enthusiasm. "Whoopee."

"Right now they're the only relatives we got," said Kerra. "And our only hope till I figure out what we're gonna do next. I don't want you making fun of them."

"Me?" said Brock innocently. "How could you think I'd do such a thing?"

"Gee, I wonder," said Kerra, sending him a crooked smile.

A dozen miles past Barstow, Kerra's eyelids starting drooping. She and Brock found a rest stop and spent the night trying to sleep with the constant sound of truckers coming and going as they stopped to use the rest rooms. Kerra tried to doze with one eye open, fearing that some evil traveler might try to get inside the car, or that a highway patrolman might roll by and check out the license plate. Surely Mr. Paulson had reported the vehicle as stolen by now.

But despite her efforts, Kerra soon found herself in deep slumber. Sometime in the middle of it all, a dream began forming in her head.

She saw in her mind a leafy, verdant forest, the sun piercing brightly through the branches. The sunlight illuminated the face of a little girl, perhaps four or five years old, in a red summer dress. There were wildflowers in her streaming blonde hair. Her eyes were alert and alive, and laughter echoed all around her as she played amidst the trees around the edges of a small clearing. Not all the laughter emanated from her. She could hear laughter from another voice. Someone was with her, but Kerra couldn't see the other face.

She was awakened by the sound of a car horn and raised her head with a start. Kerra turned to see the source—just someone in an SUV teasing his friend to hurry back from the rest room. It was morning. The sun was glowing orange in the east. Kerra glanced at her brother, still sleeping in the seat beside her, his folders of Pokemon and Yu-Gi-Oh cards snuggled in his arms. She smiled. For a kid who'd learned to hot-wire cars, Yu-Gi-Oh and Pokemon seemed like his last connections to a semi-normal childhood. Not that Kerra was any expert on the subject of normalcy. Brock restarted the car and they recommenced the journey.

Before noon they reached Las Vegas, Nevada, where Kerra purchased a meal for them at the drive-thru of Carls Jr. An hour later they passed through the Virgin River Gorge at Arizona's northwest tip, and for the first time since departing L.A., Brock looked up from his card collections to take in the towering, candy-striped cliffs on either side of the highway.

Tension was percolating inside Kerra like a coffeepot. It

was a strange kind of tension. Yes, she was anxious about finding her destination. She was nervous to think about how her relatives might react. But it was more than that. Something else was making her restless. She couldn't put a finger on it. It felt as if she were being *drawn* here, but that didn't make much sense. Her funds were dwindling fast. If her Mormon relatives didn't take her in, she wasn't quite sure what to do. She'd find a job, she supposed. She was willing to do just about anything. She and Brock could live out of the car for a few days. No big deal. Whatever happened, returning to California was not on the agenda.

As the Pontiac Sunbird crossed the border into Utah, Kerra realized that its engine sounded a little different, as if something were knocking around under the hood. *Don't quit on me now,* she whispered inwardly, almost prayerfully. *It's just a little farther.*

She bypassed the green golf courses and prim townhouses of St. George and continued on another fifteen miles until she saw the exit sign for a community called Leeds— population 412. This was it. She recognized the name. As she took the exit, her heart started pounding.

Brock pressed his face against the car window. He'd heard of towns this small, seen them in movies, but he'd never actually visited one. Leeds had only one main street, about a half mile long, lined with run down, turn-of-the-century houses, modular homes, a large building labeled The Church of Jesus Christ of Latter-day Saints, and one small diner/convenience store. No malls. No movie theaters. No arcades. The middle of nowhere. Brock spotted a young boy in a Cub Scout uniform. The kid was actually helping a little old lady across the street.

"You've gotta be kidding," he muttered under his breath.

Kerra was concentrating hard now, following a memory, a vague image from her childhood. The Pontiac's engine sounded worse than ever, like her brother's stomach after consuming an entire pepperoni pizza. She reached an inter-section with a dirt road and a hand-painted sign: *Lee Instruments 3/4 mi.* Kerra stopped the car.

"You sure you're not lost?" asked Brock.

"No," said Kerra wistfully. "This is it. I know it."

She turned the wheel. The car rumbled down the wash-board road, passing a grove of almond and cherry trees. Brock finally noticed the knocking sound in the engine.

"Is there something wrong with the car?" he asked.

Kerra didn't answer. *Just a little farther.*

Finally they reached an octagon-shaped, ramshackle shop, whitewashed, weatherworn, and surrounded by vari-ous articles more befitting to a junkyard: car engines, old fur-niture, and more than a few stray cats. Most unusual of all, however, was an old, dead juniper tree upon which hung several objects. At first Brock couldn't tell what they were. Then he figured it out. They were musical instruments—violins—glistening in the sun with a new coat of blood-red varnish.

Brock turned to his sister and asked, half seriously, "They grow on *trees?*"

Kerra smiled. "It's your grandfather's shop. He makes violins."

"My *grandfather?*" Brock repeated, as if it were an unfamiliar word, a foreign phrase that had to be carefully pronounced.

Kerra could still recall the smells—the sweet, acrid scents of exotic wood and burning resins. She could almost hear his voice, rambling on and on about re-creating the secret var-nish of Anton—Antoni—Antoni Stradman, or something like that. Funny how she could recall the old man's voice, and even almost remember the name of the old violin maker that he strove to emulate, but she could hardly remember her grandfather's face.

Kerra didn't stop. She continued driving past the shop,

past the violin tree, and past a sign that clearly read, "Private Drive." The dirt road descended into a thickly forested hollow. As the car passed through the clawing shadows of the trees, peculiar feelings were stirred up in Kerra's heart. The hollow was an eerie, hypnotic place. One of the last times she'd visited here, these woods had been under several feet of water. There'd been a flash flood. She seemed to recall someone explaining that such floods occurred every decade or so, but that the water never came up quite high enough to flood the property directly surrounding her aunt and uncle's house. Such inundations over the centuries had left a strange tangle of dead and living trees, many growing in odd, twisted directions, all of them competing violently for the light of the sun. At present the area was sprawling with undergrowth: rabbitbrush, moonflowers, thistles, and thorny mesquite, along with flourishing patches of yerba mansa whose green and crimson leaves gave the forest floor a kind of subtropical character. Wild grapes grew along the red cliffs on the left, originally planted—she couldn't believe she still remembered!—by Spanish explorers three hundred years earlier. Kerra drove very slowly, gazing into the tangled maze of branches and undergrowth.

The emotions inside her were almost rapturous. When she was a little girl her cousins used to tell her that these woods were haunted, full of mysterious shadows and voices. But Kerra had never been afraid, not even when she first came here at three or four years old. In fact, it came back to her vividly that this was one of her favorite places in the world. But why? It was just a tangle of brush. Her feelings seemed so peculiar. Yet she felt she was almost slipping into a kind of euphoric trance as her eyes searched the darkest recesses of that mysterious wood. Then all at once she brought the car to a stop.

"What's wrong?" asked Brock.

"I thought . . . I saw something," said Kerra.

Brock studied her for a moment. "Saw *what?*" His gaze now fixed on the trees.

He started to say something about Bigfoot being in California, not Utah. But before he finished the sentence, the car was jarred by a tremendous thud. Something fell onto the Pontiac's hood! Kerra shrieked, her stomach in her throat. Eyes were staring in at them through the windshield. It was a person! A *boy!* A young boy had fallen from an overhanging branch and landed directly on the hood!

The child, about eight or nine, continued to gape at them for another moment, then scrambled off the hood and ran down the wooded lane toward a partially hidden farmhouse, yelling, "Someone's here! Someone's here!"

Kerra—her nerves still recovering—pressed on the gas and rolled forward. Brock noticed that smoke was now seeping out from under the hood, but he said nothing, his mind captivated by too many other things.

The house was an eccentric mixture of Colonial and Victorian architecture with gingerbread eaves and a wrap-around porch. By the looks of it, portions of the house were still unfinished, although Kerra knew that it had been standing at least thirteen or fourteen years. Some of the porch posts were only half painted; sheets of siding still leaned against the rails, along with other building materials, all of it cradled by a decade of leaves. The rusted skeleton of an old Cadillac lay in the weeds beyond the driveway. Other ancient machines were scattered about, some appearing to be in working order, some not—motorcycle parts, farm equipment, and even an old, rusted front-end loader that Kerra remembered had been used to push back the hill that rose up sharply behind the house. It appeared that it hadn't been used since that time.

The front of the house was littered with evidence of children—dolls, Frisbees, Tonka toys, and an old, worn trampoline. As they parked the Pontiac beside an older

Maxiwagon van, the boy who'd landed on their hood disappeared inside some large French doors facing the driveway. The curtain flicked in an upstairs window. In a garage that was separated from the main part of the house, two teenage boys in greasy overalls looked up from where they were leaning over the engine of an old car. Brock recognized it— a '60s model Mustang. After all, he'd stolen one like it last winter.

Before Kerra shut off the ignition, the Pontiac let out what seemed a final gasp, sputtered, and died. The smoke seeping out from under the hood became thick and black. Kerra and Brock hesitated a moment, but at last Kerra pulled the lever to the hood and nodded for her brother to follow her. They opened their doors and went around to the front of the car. Kerra unlatched the hood and raised it. A foul-smelling puff of smoke, like a nuclear mushroom cloud, belched into the air. Kerra coughed a time or two as her brother tried to wave it off. But then their attention was immediately drawn to the screen doors along the south side of the wraparound porch.

Out stepped a middle-aged woman, stern eyes, moderately plump, with a head of bright red hair. She was wiping her hands on an apron, looking at the apparent strangers and their smoking car with more than a little curiosity. Behind the woman Kerra perceived several children of various ages. More young ones had their faces pressed to a window just right of the door.

"Gracious!" the woman exclaimed. "Are you kids lost? Can I help you?"

Kerra continued to gape as she recognized who the woman was. "Hello, Aunt Corinne," she said shyly.

The woman stopped wiping her hands. She squinted and seemed to be studying every curve and crease of Kerra's face, and also of Brock's. Her mouth opened a little, as if she might say something, but she seemed to change her mind suddenly and didn't say anything at all.

"I'm Kerra," she revealed. "I think . . . I'm your niece."

The woman's mouth fell open again, but now with a very different expression. Her eyes were filled with wonder.

"Kerra!" she declared, half in a whisper. "Oh, my word! OH, MY WORD!"

She practically flew off the porch, eyes filled with tears, and threw her arms around Kerra's shoulders. Kerra didn't realize it at first, but her own eyes were also moist, mostly out of relief, but perhaps also because a secret hope that she had nurtured for twelve years had come true. Her mother had said that they would never be welcome here again. It wasn't true. Her mother had been wrong.

A few of the children also began emerging. The two boys in the garage watched the scene, their gaze still fixed on the blonde-haired beauty with sweltering blue eyes.

One said quietly to the other, "Did she say she was my *cousin?*"

"Yeah," said his companion, smirking. "Too bad for *you*."

CHAPTER

4

"I CAN'T BELIEVE IT!" CORINNE DECLARED, her arms around both Kerra and her brother as she led them, practically carried them, into the house. "Oh, I would have never imagined! Kerra, you're so *lovely*. And *you!*" She was referring to Brock. "I haven't seen you since you were a bundle of love in your Mama's tummy."

"You're sure you don't mind us dropping in?" Kerra asked again.

"Don't be ridiculous," said Corinne. "I haven't seen my niece in twelve years and she thinks she might need an invitation?"

Brock, who hadn't yet said a word, overheard two young girls who were looking on from the bottom of the stairs.

"Their clothes smell," one whispered.

"That's just smoke," the other replied. "Like people in Las Vegas."

There were no fewer than eight children in the Whitman household, ages ranging from eighteen down to two. Kerra could only remember three kids living here when she was little. She remembered the boy, named Skyler. She also remembered the oldest girl, who was a few months younger than herself and, as she tenderly recalled, her very best friend. This girl's name had been Natasha. Another girl had been named Sherilyn. Kerra saw two strawberry-brunette teenagers who might have been them, but until they were reintroduced, she couldn't have been sure who was who.

For the past ten hours Kerra had carefully contemplated how best to approach this meeting with her relatives. Considering all that had occurred over the last twenty-four hours, it was obviously a delicate matter. The only solution, it was abundantly clear, was to lie. Later, as they sat together in the living room, Kerra explained, "Our mom got a new job in Florida. Brock and I are on our way to join her."

Corinne drew her eyebrows together. "You're traveling by yourselves?"

"Sure," said Kerra, determined not to flinch in her eye contact, though she feared she'd already glanced away more than once.

If Aunt Corinne suspected something, she didn't seem interested in pursuing it. She glanced out the window at the Pontiac, which was still emitting a little smoke from under the hood. "It appears you'll be a few days late. I'll have Skyler look it over. He's got a knack for cars and engines. When does your mother expect you?"

"A few weeks," said Kerra.

The way her aunt and older cousins widened their eyes, she feared she should have given a shorter time period. Too late to change it now.

Again, Corinne seemed to shrug it off. "Well, tonight you're staying *here*. Skyler, Teancum, help bring in their luggage."

The oldest boy, along with another boy with bright blond hair and freckles, nodded and started for the door. Brock squirmed nervously. He thought of the leather bag inside his duffel bag. Though it was unthinkable that someone might dump out his clothes and discover it, it made him nervous all the same. Finally he got up and followed after them.

At last one of the teenage brunettes presented herself. She was pretty, though shorter in height and not quite as stunning as Kerra. Thin-framed eyeglasses were perched on her tiny nose. "Kerra, do you remember me? Natasha?"

Kerra smiled brightly. "Yes. I do remember you."

Another girl, this one about fourteen, with the definite air of a tomboy, spoke up next. "How 'bout me? Sherilyn?"

"Sherilyn," Kerra repeated warmly. "The last time I saw you, you were only two or three years old."

The other children were also drawing closer, as if the actions of Natasha and Sherilyn had confirmed that it was safe.

"Now, now, don't everyone crowd her at once," said Corinne. "Girls, show her where she'll be sleeping. Brock can stay in Teancum's room. He can sleep in the bottom bunk. Colter, you sleep in your old bed in the baby's room."

"Awww," complained the boy of eight or nine who'd fallen from the tree onto the hood of the Pontiac.

Corinne couldn't resist hugging Kerra one more time. "It's so good to have you here." She grabbed some keys off the table. "I'll get your uncle from the orchard. Sherilyn, use a toothpick to check the banana bread in the oven. Tessa, Sariah—get these cats out of here."

That was another thing Kerra remembered. The Whitman household was always full of cats. A brightly colored calico was on the counter right now, licking a dirty dish.

The memories swirled in Kerra's mind like autumn leaves. So many sights, sounds, and smells. The fireman's pole was still there; it slid down from a hallway on the second story, right smack into the living room. The pole had been the pride and joy of her Uncle Drew, who'd installed it way back when he first built their house, just before Kerra was born. The imbibing scent of baking banana bread was among the other odors wafting from the kitchen. The same massive portrait of the St. George Temple hung imperiously above the couch. Kerra had once imagined it to be the castle of a rich and mysterious prince. Even the complaining squalls of the two-year-old, as Corinne carried her out the front door, seemed startlingly familiar. When Kerra was five those cries had belonged to Sherilyn. Now it was little Bernadette. She was also introduced to nine-year-old Colter, a seven-year-old girl named Tessa, and a five-year-old girl named Sariah.

Still, Kerra felt strangely uneasy, almost like a trespasser. Some of the memories associated with this place were sad and dark. It was here, in this living room, that she'd been told that her parents were going to be divorced. She'd lived with the Whitmans almost that entire summer while her mother and father fought and bickered about custody, money, and the other stuff divorcing parents fight and bicker about. This was also where she was residing when her father walked out of her life forever. She even identified the old chaise recliner where she had sat when her mother told her that Daddy was gone. Delia had explained that her father had left to pursue another life—a life without the complications and hassles of a family. She was a little girl of five, too young to understand. Too young to realize yet how much her world had changed. That was also the last day she set eyes on her aunt, uncle, and cousins.

It surprised her how well she remembered that summer's images and events. Surely human beings' memories from early childhood weren't normally so vivid. Then again, how many people had their lives turned totally upside down at the age of five? This, she guessed, was the reason so much of it was still so clear in her mind.

Kerra glanced outside and saw Brock, Teancum, and some of the other cousins unloading luggage from the comatose Sunbird. Aunt Corinne was driving away in her Maxiwagon van. Teancum offered to help Brock carry in his duffel bag, but Brock insisted on carrying it himself. Kerra heard Teancum ask him enthusiastically about the folders of Yu-Gi-Oh cards under Brock's arm. She smiled. At least the two boys would have one thing in common.

Natasha led Kerra up the stairs to her bedroom. Skyler arrived at the doorway right behind them in his greasy overalls, toting Kerra's massive trunk.

He smiled awkwardly and asked Kerra, a little out of breath, "Where do you want it?"

Natasha answered for her cousin. "Over there. She can have *my* bed."

"You've sure gotten tall," Kerra said to Skyler.

"Yeah. You too." Skyler fumbled for something more to say, then settled with, "My friend Orlan wants to meet you. He's, uh, the one who was with me in the garage—"

"Not now!" said Natasha.

She started to close the door on Skyler's nose, but not before Sherilyn slipped into the room to join them.

"Did you ever get my letters?" Natasha asked Kerra.

"Letters?" Kerra repeated.

"I must have written you ten times, back when I was seven or eight. But you never wrote back."

"I'm sorry," said Kerra. "I never got any letters."

Natasha nodded, as if this confirmed an old suspicion. "My mom said that's probably what happened. She said *your* mom didn't like us much. Oh, but I've *missed* you! My goodness, Kerra! You're so beautiful. You were *always* beautiful."

Kerra looked away and replied modestly, "That's not true."

"Oh, don't even!" said Natasha. "I bet you have *hundreds* of boyfriends."

"Nope. No boyfriends," said Kerra.

Natasha sat on the bed, patting the blanket for Kerra to sit beside her. "Tell us *everything* about California. Have you been to Disneyland?"

"Yes, I—"

"Have you swum in the ocean?" asked Sherilyn.

"*I'm* asking the questions," Natasha snapped. Then back at Kerra, "Do you know any movie stars?"

Kerra sat on the bed, a little overwhelmed. "Yes, I've swum in the ocean and no, I don't know any movie stars."

"Are you serious?" said Sherilyn. "Haven't you even *seen* any?"

"I'm afraid not."

Next Natasha asked, "Do you still talk to the Donny-Kid?"

The smile faded from Kerra's face. "Who?"

"The Donny-Kid. Don't you remember? When you were younger you used to spend hours talking to the Donny-Kid, your imaginary friend. You'd make up the wildest stories about him."

Kerra turned away, unlatching her trunk. "No. I don't do that anymore. I made all that up."

"Well, of course you did!" said Natasha. "I never thought you really believed he was real."

"The Donny-Kid?" repeated Sherilyn. "You mean like Donny the Kid? Was he a cowboy?" She giggled at an image of Donny Osmond wearing a ten-gallon hat and six-shooters.

Natasha answered. "Nah, just a little boy. A *magical* little boy. Isn't that right, Kerra?"

Kerra continued to look uncomfortable.

"I'm sorry," said Natasha. "Did I embarrass you?"

"No, no," said Kerra. "It's just been a long time since . . . since I've thought about any of that. It used to make people . . . upset."

It was an understatement. Kerra was sure it had made people think she was downright crazy. Kerra had made up Kid Donny, or the Donny-Kid, shortly after her parents had separated. Whenever she was lonely, Kid Donny was her playmate, her protector, her best friend. Kerra never felt she'd had any problem distinguishing fantasy from reality, but people around her weren't so certain. Some time later, when her mother threatened to send her to a psychiatrist, she promptly tucked her imaginary friend away and never pretended again.

"I still thought it was wonderful," Natasha persisted. "It inspired me to create my *own* imaginary friend. I called him King Cory."

"Ohh," said Sherilyn with a knowing grin. "You mean like Cory Miner?"

"No, stupid," said Natasha. "He had nothing to *do* with Cory Miner. Cory is a sleezoid. Anyway, I wanted my imaginary friend to protect me, like yours did. Never worked, though. I got frightened anyway. I guess I wasn't as creative as you."

"Frightened? What frightened you?" Kerra wondered.

"The usual. Dark closets. Bumps in the night."

"The Whistlers," added Sherilyn.

Kerra was taken aback. "Whistlers?"

Natasha scolded her sister. "You don't know what you're talking about, Sherilyn. You never heard a Whistler in your life."

"I have so."

"She's lying," said Natasha. "Nobody has heard them in practically forever."

Something jarred loose in Kerra's mind. "I remember now. The *Whistlers!*" She got up and wandered over to the bedroom window, overlooking the woods. "Oh, it's been so *long*. You really don't hear them anymore?"

"Nah," said Natasha. "Not since I was really small. Mom doesn't like us to talk about such things. She says it scares the little kids. Anyway, she used to say it was just the wind blowing through the hollow in just the right way, like holes in a flute."

"Why did it stop?" asked Kerra.

Natasha shrugged. "No one knows."

"Did *you* ever hear any Whistlers?" asked Sherilyn.

"Yes," said Kerra thoughtfully. "I-I think so."

The memory was vague, but Kerra did seem to recall . . . something. Curiously, she didn't remember it being associated with wind.

"What did it sound like?"

"I thought you said you'd heard it!" Natasha challenged.

"I *did*," said Sherilyn. "I just wanted to see if she heard the same thing."

Kerra tried to remember. "It was like . . ." Natasha and Sherilyn waited. Kerra gave up and shook her head. "I don't know."

"That's okay," said Natasha. "I don't remember it either."

Kerra turned to Sherilyn, "What did *you* hear?"

Sherilyn drew a breath to answer. Suddenly she reddened, rolled back on the bed, and threw her hands over her face, giggling. "Okay, so I never heard anything."

Natasha gave Sherilyn a "gotcha" smirk. "That's what I thought."

Sherilyn added, "But Grandpa Lee says the hollow is full of ghosts."

Natasha threw up her arms. "Great! Five minutes in our house and she already thinks we're wackos."

Kerra smiled warmly. Then she peered off toward the hollow and said, "I used to play in those woods all the time. I feel like I still remember every tree, every stone."

Natasha seemed surprised. "That's amazing. 'Cause none of us will play in there for *anything*." She was suddenly anxious to change the subject. "Are you sure you've never seen any movie stars?"

Kerra was still gazing into the shadowy forest of the hollow.

• • •

The cards were all laid out on the dining room table. Brock's collection was far more impressive than Teancum's. Nevertheless, one particular card in Teancum's pile made Brock's eyes bug out.

"You got an 'Exodia'? How?"

"Came in the original pack," said Teancum. "Mom's only bought me two."

"Two packs? She's only bought you *two packs?* And one of them had *this?*"

"Yeah. Is it valuable?"

Brock closed up his mouth. He feared he'd overplayed his enthusiasm. After settling back, he shrugged. "Oh, not . . . not *that* valuable. But, it's *pretty* good. Good for a start anyway. I got some that are a lot *more* valuable. Maybe later we can make a trade."

Brock's finagling was interrupted as the side door opened. Aunt Corinne and Uncle Drew entered the house. Brock got his first look at this uncle he'd never met. Drew's clothes were dusty, face darkly tanned, as if he'd been working a lot in the soil and sun. Drew Whitman was a skinny man, almost gaunt, but with friendly eyes and the largest hands Brock had ever seen. Brock also noticed a slight indentation on the right side of his forehead, and a diamond-shaped scar in the indentation's center.

Five-year-old Sariah jumped off the chair at the counter where she'd been tearing apart a piece of fresh banana bread and leaped into her father's arms.

"Daddy, Daddy!"

"Well, hello," said Drew, with a vague air of confusion.

Brock watched as the little girl placed her hands on both

of her father's cheeks, forcing him to look straight into her eyes.

"Sariah," she said, as if she were introducing herself to him.

Brock smirked, wondering if it was a game. At once the confusion fled from the tall man's face. He hugged his daughter deeply. "Sariah! Yes! My little one! Oh, I *love* you!"

"I love you, love you, love you too," she responded.

He set her down, and seven-year-old Tessa approached her father. "I'm Tessa."

"Hello, Tessa!" said Drew excitedly, and pulled her in for another heartfelt embrace.

Brock blinked in befuddlement. He might have thought this man had been away for *years,* as if coming home from some distant war. Brock glanced at Corinne, who sent him a subtle nod. She acted like there was something she ought to explain, but there was no time to do so now. Uncle Drew noticed Brock for the first time. Corinne made the introductions.

"This is Brock," she said.

"Brock!" said Drew. "*My boy!* How are you?"

Brock stiffened as he received a bear hug of his own.

Corinne corrected her husband. "No, honey. Brock is your *nephew*. He's Chris's boy. Chris and Delia's. You remember Delia from California?"

"Delia. Of course," said Drew rather absently. "Is that banana bread I smell?"

Drew moved toward the counter to claim a slice, releasing Brock as if there'd been no blunder, no mistake whatsoever. Brock was mortified. What was *wrong* with this guy? He'd mistaken Brock for one of his sons? He couldn't remember his own *children?* Adding to the queerness, Brock realized that he was the only one reacting as if something unusual had occurred. The other children weren't responding at all. Teancum and his nine-year-old brother, Colter, continued studying Brock's collection of cards. Seven-year-old Tessa was explaining to her mother that the second loaf of banana bread was still in the oven because the toothpick had come out "doughy."

Kerra appeared at the bottom of the stairway at the same moment that Natasha and Sherilyn made an entrance via the fire pole. Brock moved toward his sister, feeling instinctively that he needed to stand near familiar ground. Kerra noted his dazed expression.

"Are you okay?" she asked.

Brock didn't reply, just gave a jerk of the chin to indicate Uncle Drew. Natasha and Sherilyn interrupted their father in mid-bite and kissed him on the cheek, greeting him enthusiastically. They didn't bother to introduce themselves. Drew hugged them just as enthusiastically as he had the younger children. Brock began to wonder if he was imagining things. There was nothing unusual here. It was all in his mind.

"Kerra is here, Dad," said Natasha.

"Oh!" said Uncle Drew with an excitement that was starting to sound a bit mechanical, as if Kerra was just another person he should have remembered but couldn't. He stepped toward her. "Well, hello, Kerra."

"Hello, Uncle Drew," said Kerra.

As the two of them hugged, Corinne stood over her husband and explained, "Kerra is Brock's sister, honey. She's your niece."

"That's wonderful," said Drew. "Welcome! Are you staying for dinner?"

"Yes," Corinne answered for her. "Brock and Kerra are *both* staying for dinner. They'll be staying with us for a couple days."

"Fantastic. *Mi casa, su casa.* That's Spanish. Do you know what it means?"

Kerra nodded, but Drew answered anyway.

"It means my home is your home. Anything that's ours is

yours. Although I'd appreciate it if you left the family china."
He winked.

Natasha was mimicking her father, mouthing the words
as he spoke them. It was plainly a familiar joke. Several of
the children laughed. Drew tried to nab another piece of
bread.

Corinne gently slapped his hand. "Take a shower, and
dinner will be ready when you come out. No more bread!
You'll spoil your supper."

Drew said to Kerra and Brock, "She's been telling me
that since our wedding ten years ago and I haven't spoiled
it yet." He successfully snitched one more bite and escaped
toward his bedroom.

Brock did some quick math in his head. Ten years?
Clearly Aunt Corinne and Uncle Drew had been married
longer than that. He leaned toward his sister and asked in a
whisper, "What's *wrong* with him?"

Kerra curtly shook her head. This was not the time or
place.

• • •

The table was set with a large honey-cured ham, dis-
pelling any myths in Kerra's mind about Mormons and pork.
There were also church potatoes, snap peas, cucumbers
soaked in vinegar, buttermilk biscuits, and tall glasses of
whole milk. Kerra and Brock watched as everyone folded
their arms and bowed their heads for a blessing on the food.
Awkwardly, they imitated the actions, though Brock found it
very difficult to close his eyes, and peeked around at everyone often.

Five-year-old Sariah said the blessing, shutting her own
eyes as tightly as canning lids. "Dear Heavenly Father," she
began, "we thank Thee for this day, and for my kittens, and
my horse, and my Barbies—"

Seven-year-old Tessa decided she needed some coaching. She whispered, *"and bless the food . . ."*

Sariah looked up at her. "Not yet!" She lowered her head again and continued. "And for Brock and . . ." She looked up again. "What's her name?"

"Kerra," Corinne and several of the children said simultaneously.

"And for Kerra. And hope they can visit us again. And hope we can set a good 'sample like Mommy says. And hope their car gets better. And hope we don't find out they're in trouble with the law . . ."

Both Aunt Corinne's and Kerra's eyes popped open at that.

" . . . And bless the food. In the name of Jesus Christ. Amen."

An awkward silence persisted after the prayer, but only for a second. Then Aunt Corinne promptly asked for someone to pass the cucumbers.

Kerra and Brock answered many more questions about life for a boy and girl growing up in California. Corinne also asked some questions about Delia and the move to Florida. Kerra answered with as few words as possible. She didn't like to lie. She was certain she wasn't very good at it. Brock noted that Uncle Drew acted fairly normal through dinner, though he did seem much more inclined to listen than to ask questions.

Later that night, Brock and Kerra found a moment alone in Teancum's bedroom. As they sat on the bottom bunk, Brock finally wheedled an explanation from his sister about Uncle Drew.

"He was injured," Kerra explained. "It happened the summer that our parents were divorced. If I remember right, he had some sort of accident in a machine shop. A metal rod hit him right here." She indicated the spot on her own forehead where Drew's scar was located on his. "I think they said part of it is still inside him."

Brock's winced. "Inside his *brain?* So is he like a zombie?"

"Of course not," said Kerra. "He still owns a really big orchard for almonds and cherries. I think he still runs it. Does he *seem* like a zombie?"

"No, but . . ."

"It just affected his memory."

"Affected it how?"

"I'm not quite sure," said Kerra.

"It affected his *short-term* memory," said a voice from the doorway. It was Sherilyn. A toothbrush with blue and white toothpaste on the bristles was in her hand. She'd been eavesdropping. She seemed proud to be able to repeat such a sophisticated phrase.

From their expressions it was clear that Brock and Kerra didn't understand. Sherilyn was only too happy to elaborate. "It's like that one fish in the movie *Finding Nemo,* except the movie didn't really get it right. It means my dad can remember things that happened a long time ago. He just can't remember things that happened yesterday. Or even an hour ago. In fact, he has a hard time remembering *anything* that's taken place since the accident."

"Has it gotten . . . worse over the years?" asked Kerra.

Sherilyn shrugged. "Seems about the same to me. At least he knows who *I* am—most of the time. He remembers Skyler and Natasha, too. But the little ones, they have to remind him every single day."

"Every single day?" asked Brock incredulously.

"They're used to it," said Sherilyn a little defensively. "We're *all* used to it. He remembers things best when he gets excited. When that happens, I'll bet he could name every state capital and every president in one breath." She noted Brock and Kerra's expressions and added sincerely, "My dad

loves everybody. And everybody loves him. He hugs everyone he meets. It doesn't matter who—even strangers. I guess
he's afraid he might already know them and he doesn't want
to be embarrassed. It's funny, I guess, but I think it's sorta
cool too. Well, good night." Sherilyn started brushing her
teeth as she walked off.

"I think it's *weird*," Brock whispered after he was sure
she was gone. "This whole *family* is weird. Like the Brady
Bunch on a million gallons of caffeine. I can't take it. I gotta
get outa here."

"Don't sweat it," said Kerra. "We won't stay long."

"They know somethin's up," said Brock. "They'll turn us
in."

"I don't think so. Besides, right now we can't go anywhere. We have nowhere else to turn."

"I'll steal another car—"

"No," said Kerra sternly. "I don't want us doing any more
of that. *Ever!*"

"I want to go home," said Brock forlornly.

"To what?" asked Kerra. "There's nothing for us. I
thought you were getting along well with Teancum. He has
Yu-Gi-Oh cards, doesn't he?"

"One good card. These people are hicks! No Nintendo.
No Sega. Have you seen their videos and DVDs? Disney,
Disney, Disney, Disney—*Ahhh!* I'm going insane!" Brock lay
back on the bed, convulsing and flailing as if going through
some kind of electric shock.

Kerra watched, unmoved. "Are you finished?"

Brock stopped convulsing, but replied, "No."

Kerra laughed. She wrapped her arms around her
brother's shoulders. "We'll be okay. We can survive a few
days."

"No, we can't," said Brock.

"Yes, we can," said Kerra.

"No, we can't."

Kerra kissed the top of her brother's head. "Yes," she said softly. "We can."

• • •

Corinne sat on the porch swing with her husband. The evening was cool, and it appeared that most of the children had gone to bed. Drew was looking off at the moon, blazing brightly in the sky even though it wasn't quite dark enough for most stars.

"Maybe I should call their mother," said Corinne, more to herself than to Drew.

"Good idea," Drew replied.

Corinne was perfectly aware that Drew likely didn't know what she was talking about. She knew he'd already forgotten Kerra and Brock's names and would have to be reminded tomorrow. But this had been the pattern of Corinne Whitman's life for more than a decade, and she was used to it. In fact, she loved her husband no less, and even enjoyed conversing with him. Yes, it could be frustrating discussing matters with any kind of history behind them. Still, she was astonished how profound his responses and his bits of advice usually were. Often Drew said what he said simply out of pride, not wanting to admit that he didn't fully understand. But there were times—precious, blessed times—when Corinne was convinced that the Spirit illuminated his clouded mind and led him to say exactly what she needed to hear.

"They say Delia doesn't have a phone yet at her apartment in Florida." Corinne sighed dismally. "Then again, even if I *could* call her . . ."

"What do you mean?" asked Drew. "Why couldn't you?"

Corinne was silent for a moment. She wasn't sure Drew still recalled all the ill feelings of their last meeting with Delia. It was right after her brother had gone away. Delia

McConnell had almost seemed *relieved* that Chris had disappeared, as if it proved that her opinion of her ex-husband had been accurate all long. As if it validated all the awful things she'd said and done. But Corinne had an entirely different perspective of the matter.

She finally replied to her husband, "I guess I just don't want to muddy the waters. I'm gonna enjoy my niece and nephew while I can. A phone call might spoil it."

"You still blame her, don't you?" said Drew.

Corinne looked at him in surprise. It was one of those inexplicable, lucid moments. She knew by experience not to try to verify if he really understood what he'd said. It would suddenly seem like he was making a statement that belonged in a conversation from twenty years ago. Corinne had to take it for what it was. And in the present context, she knew *precisely* what it meant.

"Perhaps I do," said Corinne. "I *do* blame Delia." She gazed off into the night. A shadow of pain and resentment moved over her heart. She said bitterly, "My brother didn't abandon his family. She *did it,* Drew. Or if not, she knows who did. She got away with murder. All these years . . ." Her voice trailed off.

The yip of a coyote echoed somewhere off in the hills. Drew did not reply for a long time. Then at last he looked at his watch. "Hey, we ought to go to bed. Don't you think, my love?"

Corinne gazed again at Drew's face. The innocence she saw in those eyes instantly frightened away any shadow of resentment.

She kissed his cheek. "Yes. I think we should."

5

KERRA AWAKENED TO THE sweet melody of a mockingbird in the umbrage of the hollow. The cooing had a consoling, reassuring effect that made her content to just lie there under the covers of Natasha's bed and bask in it for a while. A few moments later, she heard the voices of her aunt and uncle from the living room, the sound wafting up through the hole around the fire pole.

"You didn't have to get dressed," Drew said to his wife. "I'll drive myself this morning."

"I'll drive, I'll drive," said Corinne in a tired but steady voice. "We go through this every morning. If you drove yourself, I'd never see you again. Now it's Friday, so you'll be in the north acre. Make sure that . . ."

Her voice faded away as the front door opened and shut. Kerra decided to emerge from her nest of blankets. She wandered over to the window to watch Corinne and Drew pull away, their van disappearing into the canopy of trees. The morning was mostly overcast, but there must have been a hole in the clouds of the eastern sky behind her, because it seemed as if a golden beam illuminated the hollow and the rocky hillside to the west. She was peering into the woods again.

And listening.

Nevertheless, she heard only the mockingbird, along with a half dozen other melodic birds that she couldn't have named. Kerra shut her eyes and breathed it in, drawing it all deep inside her. Then, as if startled by a new and mischievous idea, she quickly dressed and slipped her shoes on her feet. She descended the stairs—quietly, because no one else was stirring. Then she opened the front door and descended into the fresh, glittering morning.

Kerra crossed the driveway and entered the woods, kicking her feet through the crimson leaves of yerba mansa. The clouds seemed to be breaking up. She closed her eyes and let the odors of mesquite and sage and the pollens of a million wildflowers draw her forward. When she opened them again, she heard the chitter of several quails. Her eyes spotted a few escaping across the forest floor—a mother with a brood of four or five chicks. Her gaze traveled up the trunks of several black willows and cottonwoods, the twisted and tangled branches painting gossamer webs of shadow and sunlight on every surface. Oh, it was a magical place! She concentrated hard to try and hear those whistles and whispers that Sherilyn and Natasha had spoken of. But except for birds and the rustle of her own steps, the woods were perfectly silent.

But so full of memories! A *symphony* of memories! These tangled trees seemed much smaller now, despite the fact the foliage was so thick that sometimes she could hardly see the blue of the sky. As a little girl she'd felt certain that if she walked far enough into these woods she could become lost here forever in a world of fantasy and fairies and magical kingdoms.

She passed through the remains of an old corral that

likely hadn't kept horses for fifty years. Foolish settlers must have built it before they understood about the decennial flash floods. Now all that was left standing were a few ragged fences, weathered wood, rusted barbwire, and an aged, plastic sign with white and red letters that read, "No Hunting/No Trespassing." Kerra almost gasped in delight. She *knew* that sign. She knew it like an old, dear friend. Knew from a time before she could even *read!* Uncle Drew had posted it in the days before his accident to discourage sportsmen seeking deer, pheasant, and rabbit. Just as she'd done more than a decade before, Kerra ignored the sign and wandered into the deeper, thicker woods beyond.

The farther she walked, the more alert she became. The crunching of twigs began to seem more pronounced, more isolated from all other sounds. She pushed her way through a thicket of scratchy branches overgrowing the path, only vaguely aware of her destination. She knew only that it was a secret, hidden place where she had played as a little girl. What, she asked herself, was drawing her here? It was all so foggy, so uncertain, as if memory itself were calling, beckoning.

The beat of her heart soon dwarfed even the crunch of twigs. A nervous tension seeped into her veins. Suddenly the gnarled trees seemed *exactly* as large as she remembered, brooding and ominous. The area had no evidence of human interference. Not a fence post, an old rusted can, or even a gum wrapper. It was as if she'd crossed some sort of boundary into a prehistoric realm. She felt wholly and utterly alone. Yet she pushed on, and at last the place she sought crept into view.

It was a clearing. Not a wide clearing—perhaps only twenty or thirty feet all around. Its edges were guarded by thistles and brambles of mesquite. An old, massive cottonwood had fallen completely on its side to the right. But despite the cottonwood's fate, several branches along the upward side of its trunk continued to produce thousands of green, living leaves, as if this clearing had the power to grant life to dying things. So many years ago Kerra had felt this place had the same exact effect upon her.

The tenseness inside her remained, and her heart thumped like a timepiece. Was it fear that she felt? She scoffed at herself. Only moments ago her heart had leapt with indescribable elation. What had changed? What could possibly make her feel afraid?

She moved aside some weeds and found the stone. It almost surprised her when it appeared—the same rusty red color with white colored lichen. This was where she used to sit. Obviously no one else had sat here for twelve long years. The thought made her sad.

Kerra shook herself. Wow, what emotion was next? She'd certainly gone the gamut this morning. But the waterfall of memories hadn't ended. Like the night before last, she saw in her mind a little girl in a red summer dress. She heard laughter as this girl danced and played in the glowing light of the green woods. Only now she remembered something new.

It was a feather—a feather from an exotic bird that she couldn't name. Its colors were gorgeous—glittering blue and green. This feather floated in her mind's eye, hovering. She felt as if she could see the little girl holding out her hand, but the feather seemed to penetrate right through her fingers, landing softly at her feet. This only caused the little girl to laugh all the more. The little girl looked up. She was looking at someone. In her mind Kerra strained to see the face. Who was the little girl looking at?

All at once she felt the need to back away, return to the clearing's edge where she could take in the whole location again. As she was in the act of turning, her eyes met another human face. But it wasn't the face she expected. Kerra gasped from the pit of her stomach.

It was an old man. The hair on his head was hoary like

November frost. His beard still had a bit of brown, but it was mostly grizzled white, sort of like a Kodiak bear. He wore a dark green plaid shirt and light gray-blue suspenders that were the same color as his eyes. After a moment of recovery, Kerra realized at last who it was. Her memory was completely restored. Oddly, he looked hardly a day older than when she'd last laid eyes on him.

"A lot has changed," the old man said, taking in the woods and the clearing, as if he'd stood in this place before but hadn't visited it for a long time. He approached Kerra and said, almost dreamily, "Twelve years ago a flood washed through here. That's when it stopped."

"You're . . . Grandpa Lee," said Kerra, a little breathless.

"Yup. And you must be Sakerra. The little girl who used to practically live among these trees like a woodland fairy. Am I right?"

Kerra nodded. "You frightened me."

"I do that a lot," said Grandpa Lee. "Your grandmother told me I did it to her all the time. God rest her. I was coming down the driveway and I saw you enter the woods. I figured this was where you might be headed."

"No one has called me Sakerra in forever."

Grandpa Lee came closer. "Your father named you that. *Little Cherry Blossom.* It's Japanese, I think."

Kerra remembered that before her parents had divorced, *everyone* had called her that. But her mother didn't care for the name. Kerra wasn't even sure if any official record listed her as that, except maybe her hospital birth certificate. It sounded so peculiar and yet invigorating to hear it now.

"How did you know this was where I was headed?" Kerra asked.

"'Cause somehow I was usually the one sent out to search for you. I found you here more than once."

"What do you mean, 'That's when it stopped'?"

"The sound of the Whistlers," said Grandpa Lee mysteriously. "The shadows that flit and skirt through these woods. The voices and spirits of the dead. Flood must have thrown things out of kilter somehow."

"I don't understand," said Kerra.

"That's 'cause I'm tryin' to make it sound as spooky as I can. How am I doin'?" Grandpa Lee teasingly wriggled his fingers in the air and made a silly off-key howl, like a Halloween ghost. Afterwards he started laughing.

Kerra smiled, blushing slightly.

"Now look at that," said Grandpa Lee, pointing at Kerra's face. "*There* she is. *There's* the little girl I remember, right there in that smile."

Tears came to Kerra's eyes. She hugged her grandfather and started to cry.

Grandpa Lee returned the embrace and asked, "Now, what's this?"

"I don't know," said Kerra, wiping a tear. "I guess I . . . I didn't know . . . I didn't realize how much I *missed* everything."

Grandpa Lee beamed. "I have something for you up in my shop. It's hot, and I'll bet you know exactly what it is."

Kerra nodded. "I do. *Exactly.*"

A half hour later she was nestled among the benches and tools of her grandfather's violin shop, plopping a marshmallow into a frothing cup of hot chocolate. Not a *mini*-marshmallow, but a full campfire-sized specimen that threatened to send the drink flowing over the edges. But Kerra knew precisely how to bob it gently up and down with her fingernail, slowly dissolving it in the heat.

The smells of turpentine, raw cedar, spruce, and maple were as pronounced as Kerra had ever remembered. Over her head hung rows and rows of wood blocks precisely sixteen inches long, five inches wide, and one inch thick. The wood came from trees that grew as far away as the Tyrolean

Alps in Switzerland and as close as Cedar Mountain north-east of Cedar City, Utah. Some of it had been drying, or cur-ing, for as long as twenty years. Each piece of wood was destined to become the front or back, neck or fingerboard, of Lee McConnell's violins.

"I remember sitting here for hours," said Kerra, "watch-ing you carve, or mixing your secret varnishes."

Grandpa Lee got a twinkle in his eye, as if he were hid-ing a great secret. "Got something to show you."

He opened a black velvet case and revealed a beautiful red instrument with a sheen to the wood that made it look as deep as a glass prism.

"This is it," said Grandpa Lee. "You're looking at as fine an instrument as has been made in the last three hundred years. I *did* it, Sakerra. I perfected the amber varnish of Antonio Stradivari. In fact, I *bettered* it. The sheen on this vio-lin will still look as beautiful a thousand years after Stradivari's best have faded. I promise you, here's an instrument that would make them *all* proud—Stradivari, Guarneri, Amati. And the *sound*. Just listen."

He pulled it carefully from the case, propped it against his neck, and let the bow glide along the strings. He played the first few notes of "Variations on a Theme by Paganini" by Rachmaninoff, and Kerra listened in dreamy fascination as every corner and niche of the cramped shop was filled with a sound as sweet and stirring as any music under heaven. She knew a little about classical music—had often tuned her radio to just those stations. But perhaps what she knew most was *sound*. It was something no one had taught her. She just knew it. Grandpa finished with a flourish, then looked at Kerra. He looked at her as if her opinion meant everything in the world.

"It's beautiful!" said Kerra sincerely. "One of the most gorgeous sounds I've ever . . . Are you going to sell it?"

Grandpa Lee's face mellowed. He looked down and

shuffled a bit as he laid the instrument back into its case. "Well, my little Sakerra. That's a complicated question. Violin making is a complicated game, and very political. You see, I'm still alive. No one really respects a *living* maker. It's like most works of art. Before it can truly be worth something, the artist has to die. Perhaps someday *you* could sell it for me."

"Me?" said Kerra in surprise. "Oh no, Grandpa. I could never—"

"Oh, yes, you could. You have the gift, my girl. Even when you were little you could hear things that not many others can hear. I can tell. I could *always* tell. It's the same gift that draws you to those woods."

Kerra raised her eyebrows. "You think I'm drawn to the woods because of a *gift?*"

Grandpa smirked a little, as if he wanted to come across a little less seriously. "*I* think so. Those woods are an ancient place. That whole hollow. This whole *area,* as a matter of fact. The Indians knew it. They were still coming here to pray when I was a kid. I can't explain it. Maybe it's the fault line that runs along the base of the ridge. Or a combination of things. It's all pulled together right here. History. Voices. Everything that's ever happened. Not only here, but . . . well . . . on this whole continent."

Kerra's blank expression made it clear she wasn't following.

Grandpa Lee added, "Prophets have said that this land was once home to a people as noble as any who ever walked the earth, as well as those equally as evil."

"Prophets said this? What prophets?"

"Nephi and Moroni. Brigham Young, Heber C. Kimball. Modern prophets said several interesting things about this very country and its little communities: Harrisburg, Leeds, Silver Reef, St. George—"

"Oh, you mean *Mormon* prophets," said Kerra.

He seemed to realize in an instant that Kerra knew nothing about these things, and she could tell that it disappointed him deeply, as if she *should* have known, but someone had let her down. "Yes, *Mormon* prophets," Grandpa Lee repeated. "But *you* feel it too, don't you? You can feel their presence. Hear their voices, like echoes from the past. I know *I* can sometimes. Especially in those woods."

He saw a change in Kerra's countenance. She was suddenly edgy and nervous. "I don't think *that's* what I feel."

"You don't?" The old man watched her another moment, then sighed, "Well, maybe you don't. Maybe I don't either. But you must admit, imagination can be a sweet thing. A comforting thing. Yes, a very comforting thing."

Kerra smiled again. Her grandfather looked weary all of a sudden, and quite lonely. She realized he'd been alone for a very long time. His wife had died before Kerra was born.

Kerra sipped her hot chocolate and let her mind drift off—off into the sweet comfort of her imagination.

● ● ●

Spree felt sure that he'd heard a noise.

He stared out the window of his cousin's East Los Angeles home into the darkened street, careful to stand far to one side, preventing his silhouette from becoming an easy target. He was alone tonight. His cousin hadn't yet come home, and Spree, in his paranoia, was starting to think it was because his cousin had ratted him out—that he'd told Hitch where Spree was hiding.

Spree was shaking so badly he could hardly grip the knife in his right hand, and he was all out of cigarettes to help calm his nerves. By now the Shamans certainly knew what he had stolen. Spree could also be sure that they would search for him. What he didn't realize—what he hadn't planned for—was the feeling that there was nowhere on earth where he could feel safe. All evening he'd been tormented by the notion that he might never feel safe again.

The noise wasn't in his imagination. He was certain that he'd heard someone walking along the side of the house. He also swore that he'd heard whispering. Yet Spree saw nothing in the dark shadows beneath the streetlights—nothing along the rickety wooden fence on the south side of the property.

He decided he couldn't take this anymore. He was getting out of here. But where could he go? He couldn't leave! This was where he'd told the kid to call him! It would all be pointless if he wasn't here to receive that call. *Where was Brock?! Why hadn't he called?!*

His cousin had an answering machine. Spree decided he ought to leave for a few hours, buy more cigarettes, and come back to see if there was a message. Maybe he *was* overly jittery. Maybe the sounds and the whispers were all in his mind. But either way, he was sure that if he could just get out for a little while, he'd feel much better.

Yet Spree had not quite reached the front door before it smashed open under the heavy boot of Hitch Ventura. In rushed four of the most vicious members of the Shaman gang—Hitch, Adder, Prince, and Dushane. Spree turned and fled toward the back bedroom. There was a window. He tried to dive through the screen. But Adder and Dushane were right behind him. They yanked him back in and pinned him hard against the wall. Spree still had the knife—he could have tried to fight back. But his flaccid spine was connected directly to the muscles of his wrist, and he dropped the knife onto the floor.

Hitch glowered down on him. "Where is it?"

"Where's what?" Spree asked. "What are you talking ab—?"

"You know *exactly* what I'm talkin' about."

"No, I swear. You can search the place. Search anywhere. I don't got it, Hitch."

Hitch slapped his face. "You must think I'm pretty stupid. You disappoint me, man."

Without hesitation, Hitch removed a 38-Special from his belt behind his back and pressed the barrel into Spree's temple. The game was over. Spree's body turned to jelly. Adder and Prince struggled to hold him upright.

"*Wait!*" Spree screeched. "*Please! Don't do it!* It was the kid! I gave it to the kid!"

This confirmed suspicions that Hitch had had all along. He'd already checked back at Brock and Kerra's apartment. He'd asked everyone he could think of, but no one seemed to know what had become of them.

"The kid is gone," said Hitch. "Where is he?"

"I don't know," said Spree, blubbering like a walrus. As Hitch again pressed the gun into his temple, he cried, "*I swear it!* They left town! But he's supposed to call."

"Call?" said Adder. "Here?"

"Yes," said Spree.

"When?" Hitch demanded.

"Anytime. I swear it, Hitch. I s-swear."

At last they let their former comrade sink to the floor, him having lost control of both tear ducts and bowels.

Hitch looked hungrily at the phone on the night table.

• • •

Corinne glanced through the kitchen window, her fingers encrusted in pizza dough as she faithfully kneaded it the required number of times for maximum rising. Kerra was outside by the garage, leaning over the engine of the Pontiac Sunbird. Beside her were Skyler and his friend Orlan. Just looking at their faces, Corinne could tell that the prognosis was not good. Fixing Kerra's vehicle would assuredly be an expensive undertaking. Even if they got it running, Corinne didn't feel good at all about allowing Kerra and Brock to drive it more than two thousand miles to Florida. But what could Corinne say about it? Apparently their mother had approved of the expedition, though Corinne was starting to wonder just how much Delia knew about what was going on.

Just as she decided in her mind to insist that Kerra give her some sort of address or phone number so she could speak with Delia personally, the phone let out a pealing ring. Corinne looked around for a towel to wipe the dough from her hands, then gave up in frustration and grabbed the handset.

"Hello?" she said.

"Mrs. Whitman?" said a male voice.

"Speaking."

The voice seemed to pause, almost in relief, as if a difficult search had finally produced positive results. "My name is Carson Paulson. I'm with California Welfare and Family Services. We're looking for your niece and nephew, Kerra and Brock McConnell. Your name wasn't listed in any of their files, but we did some digging and—"

Corinne was taken aback. "Are they in trouble?"

"Um . . . yes," the man confirmed. "I'm afraid so. They stole a car, Mrs. Whitman, and . . . uh, escaped our custody. There's a warrant out. I know the children have been upset since their mother's death. But these are serious charges and—"

Stunned, Corinne interrupted. "Delia is *dead?*"

The man's voice suddenly sounded very awkward. "Yes. I'm sorry. I thought you would have known. The children were in the state's custody. I had hoped, maybe, that you might have seen or heard from them. It's possible that—"

"I have to go," said Corinne.

"Excuse me?" said Mr. Paulson. "Mrs. Whitman?"

Corinne quickly hung up the phone. Then she stood

there, gaping at it. What had she just done? Or a better question: What was she going to do now?

She took a minute to collect her wits, then finally washed the dough from her hands and wiped flour off the handset.

When she went outside, Kerra was on the porch, leaning on the railing, watching the children jump on the trampoline. Brock and Teancum were bouncing together, trying to throw one another off balance while the others laughed and cheered them on. Corinne braced herself and approached, though she still had no idea what she was going to say.

Kerra nodded toward her brother and remarked, "I thought he'd forgotten how to be a kid."

Corinne studied her niece for a moment, then said, "You probably haven't had much of a chance to be a kid yourself, have you, Kerra?"

Kerra shrugged, then looked off toward some imaginary horizon. "It's just luck, I guess. The way things happen. The way they are."

Corinne leaned on the railing beside her and said philosophically, "But the way things finally *turn out*—we all have a say in that. Wouldn't you agree? God willing?"

Kerra looked doubtful as she turned up a corner of her mouth. "I'm afraid I'm not very religious."

Thoughtfully, Corinne replied, "Maybe you just need something worth believing in."

Kerra let this sink in, then said, "My dad was a Mormon, right?"

Corinne sensed the bitterness in her voice, the sideways challenge Kerra was posing. She frowned and said painfully, "Your dad loved you, Kerra. I know you may have been told many things, but . . ."

Immediately Kerra changed the subject. "I was wondering, Aunt Corinne . . . if you knew of any jobs. For the summer, I mean."

Corinne suspected that Skyler had given Kerra some kind

of damage estimate on the car. "Perhaps. What about Florida?"

"Mom's not quite settled in," Kerra replied after only the slightest pause. "I'm sure she'd think it was fine."

The young girl didn't make eye contact. Didn't or *couldn't.*

"If you need any help, Kerra," said Corinne soberly, "any help at all, I'll be there for you. Any way I can."

Kerra finally looked at her aunt. Almost as quickly she broke eye contact. "Thank you."

Corinne studied her niece's face as she continued watching the children on the trampoline.

● ● ●

The following day was Sunday. It was the first time Kerra had visited any kind of church in the last twelve years. She borrowed a dress from Natasha, though it fit rather tightly and came to the top of her knees (although Skyler's friend, Orlan, commented that it fit her just fine). Brock got a white shirt from Teancum. The boys struggled in vain to tie a proper knot in Brock's tie, a dilemma resolved by the able hands of Uncle Drew. Again Brock had to remind him that he was not one of his children.

The two orphans suffered through sacrament meeting with dull expressions, understanding very little and enjoying even less. Brock refused to be separated from Kerra during Sunday School, despite their age difference. He consented to go with Teancum during the last half of Primary, but refused to sing a single note about "popcorn popping on apricot trees" or "Lemon-ites in ancient history," whatever the heck a Lemon-ite was.

Brock felt relieved when they all arrived back at the farmhouse around four o'clock in the afternoon, but perplexed when he couldn't talk *anyone* into going outside to play on the tramp or ride the four-wheeler on such a beautiful summer day.

"It's the Sabbath," Sherilyn explained.

"You mean everyone just stays in the house and watches TV?" asked Brock.

"Actually," said Teancum, "Mom doesn't like the TV on on Sunday either. But we could play games."

"What kind of games?" asked Brock.

"Lots of 'em. Bible Quest, Missionary Impossible, Celestial Pursuit, Tennis Shoes Among the Nephites—"

"Not that one," said Sherilyn. "The questions are too hard."

"What about Yu-Gi-Oh?" asked Brock.

Teancum seemed apprehensive. "I guess it would be all right."

Brock smiled broadly. "Then step right this way . . ." The boys disappeared upstairs.

After a late meal fit for Thanksgiving and an evening's conversation with Aunt Corinne, Uncle Drew, and Natasha, Kerra started upstairs for bed and noticed Teancum glumly sitting on the bottom step.

"Where's Brock?" she inquired.

"Upstairs."

"I thought you two were playing games."

"We were. He won all my cards."

"He *what?*"

"All my Yu-Gi-Oh. All my Pokemon. He won them all."

Kerra's hands clenched into fists; the blood rushed to her face. Angrily, she stomped upstairs and found the culprit on the bottom bunk in Teancum's bedroom, gloating over his winnings.

"Give them back," Kerra gruffed.

"Give *what* back?" asked Brock innocently.

"You know very well. I can't *believe* you took advantage of your cousin."

67

Brock's mouth twisted into a smile. "Aw, I was gonna give 'em back anyway. Here. You can give them back for me." He handed over a stack of cards.

"Is this all?"

"Yep. Practically."

"Don't lie to me, Brock. Is this all or not?"

"I'll even throw in two of mine," said Brock.

"Is this all or isn't it?"

"I won his cards fair and square. I have a right to keep just one."

"Give it over."

"No," said Brock.

Kerra saw the card in question behind him on the blanket. He tried to hide it with his arm.

"Give me that card!"

"I won't!"

Kerra lunged forward, diving for the glittering "Exodia" Yu-Gi-Oh card. Brock seized it first, then threw his body over the top of it. Kerra dug her nails into the flesh of Brock's arms. They rolled out of the bunk, wrestling on the floor. At last Kerra bent her brother's arm painfully behind his back. Her fingers were pinching the card's corner. She forced him to let go. As Kerra got to her feet, she saw that the card was now bent and slightly torn.

"Look what you did!" Brock shouted.

"You'll give him one of your own to replace it. Whichever one he chooses." Kerra snatched up Brock's binder. She turned to leave.

"I hate you!" she heard as she slammed the door. *"I hate you!"*

Kerra started toward the stairs. She had just placed her foot on the second step—

And then it struck.

CHAPTER

6

THE GROUND STARTED RUMBLING—a low trembling that seemed removed from audible sound, as if it originated from *within* the ear, spreading outward. Kerra's legs felt unsteady, like she was walking on foam. She looked down the stairway, contemplating the potentially nasty fall and she grasped the railing for support, dropping her brother's binder of *Yu-Gi-Oh* cards. At the base of the stairs she saw several objects teeter off a bookshelf. Elsewhere something shattered, and she heard the shriek of Tessa and the yelp of her Aunt Corinne.

The lights blinked once, then fizzled out entirely, leaving Kerra enveloped in surprising darkness. *Primeval* darkness. She continued to grip the rail, now out of fear as much as to maintain her balance. For a fraction of an instant, Kerra felt sure the world had come to an end.

The rumbling concluded, but a queer uneasiness lingered, as if the ground were swimming in several directions at once. Then even this sensation faded, leaving only the darkness. Kerra heard the cries of her younger cousins—cries coming from several places in the house. She heard the frantic voice of her uncle: "Is everyone all right? Is anyone hurt?"

Footsteps scrambled up the stairs.

"Uncle Drew?!" whimpered Kerra.

"Take my hand," he said.

"Brock!" Kerra shouted. "*Brock!*"

"I'm here!" came the reply.

Her uncle grasped her elbow. Seconds later Brock latched onto her waist. Uncle Drew led them both to safety.

According to station KDXU, St. George, Utah, the earthquake measured 4.9 on the Richter scale. The epicenter was approximately one mile northeast of Leeds. No damage had yet been reported, but a more detailed assessment would be made in the morning. When the announcer's voice started to fade, Uncle Drew reached over and cranked his hand-generated flashlight/radio. Kerra was amazed. She'd never seen such an invention—didn't even know it existed.

"Four-point-nine," Brock scoffed. "That's nothin.'" Having grown up in Los Angeles, he considered himself the presiding expert.

"Didn't *feel* like nothin,'" said Teancum.

"One mile northeast of Leeds," Skyler repeated. "That's right underneath us!"

The entire family was gathered in the front room downstairs, their faces illuminated by the flicker of a dozen candles. Little Bernadette and Sariah were both asleep on the couch on either side of Aunt Corinne. Colter was sleeping alongside his sister Tessa. The rest had remained awake throughout the vigil, sleep chased away by adrenaline. They'd just experienced a real-life, honest-to-goodness earthquake!

"Not quite as big as the one in '92," Uncle Drew commented. "That one was 5.8. But the epicenter was twenty miles south, so this one *felt* stronger."

Her uncle's memory was much keener than usual, Kerra

noted. Sherilyn's comment that he remembered things better when he got excited appeared to be accurate.

As far as anyone could determine, the only damage in the home was a cracked flower vase. Other items had fallen off shelves and counters, and the portrait of the St. George Temple now sat askew, but nothing else appeared to have broken. Uncle Drew and Skyler took some flashlights and ventured up to the shop to check on Grandpa Lee. Then they surveyed the outside of the property looking for structural damage. They found nothing, but expressed a desire to check it again in daylight.

After another couple hours even the most exhilarated of Kerra's cousins grew bleary-eyed. All the candles but one were extinguished. Aunt Corinne and Uncle Drew retired to their bedroom with several of the youngest family members, who were eagerly insisting that they be allowed to sleep with them in their king-size bed. Kerra, Brock, Skyler, Teancum, Natasha, and Sherilyn—anyone with bedrooms upstairs—gathered pillows and blankets into the front room and slept in tangled heaps on the couches and chairs.

Kerra never really did fall into any kind of deep slumber. Something peculiar was tingling inside her. She couldn't place what it was or what it meant. But the feeling made her restless, and the best she could do was doze.

She was in just such a state, not even unconscious enough to dream, when the kitchen light flickered on. Kerra roused and looked about. Many of the house lights had illuminated—every light that had been on at the moment when the electricity had cut out. The front room itself, however, remained quite dim, the brightest thing being the glow of the digital clock on the VCR. No one around her had awakened.

She couldn't have known the hour—the VCR read its default time of 12:00. As she peered though the front window, she perceived a vaguely lit morning sky. It was perhaps

71

a little after six A.M. Kerra climbed out from under her blanket and stood. She was still dressed in the jeans and shirt she'd put on yesterday after church. She needed only to slip her shoes on her feet. Brock was snoring obliviously. So was Teancum. She again focused on the pale light coming through the front room window. All at once, her eyebrows drew together. There was something peculiar about the light, something odd about . . .

As Kerra took several steps toward the window, she realized it wasn't the light. It was the *sound*. Urgently, she approached the front door. Kerra threw it open and moved out onto the porch. No air would go into her lungs, as if the oxygen had been sucked away from the earth and it was now an airless planet. Her heart raced; her mind was a blizzard of anxiety and wonder.

The sound!

It was the sound! The one from her childhood. The sound that Sherilyn and Natasha had mentioned. The sound that had once dominated the hollow when all was quiet, but had disappeared after the last flash flood. Just hearing it for an instant brought it all back.

"*The Whistlers*," Kerra uttered under her breath.

But what did that mean? Was it really a whistle? To Kerra it seemed more like a *whisper*. Actually, it was neither of these. It was a low, droning whir, higher pitched than the wings of a cricket. But it wasn't exactly a drone, either. It almost seemed to echo, amplify, and fade—just like a whisper.

But was it really a sound at all? Or was it some sort of vibration? Kerra couldn't decide. She was certain of only one thing: Natasha's statement that it was created by wind blowing just right through the trees, like holes in a flute, was entirely inaccurate. No leaves were fluttering. The hollow was as still as a cathedral's inner sanctum. The sound had nothing whatsoever to do with wind.

Kerra drew her first breath in what had seemed like

minutes. She was trembling like a leaf. Every instinct told her to remain where she stood, yet Kerra refused to obey. She stepped off the porch, crossed the driveway, and entered the shadowy undergrowth of the hollow.

The trees loomed like phantoms, menacing sorcerers cloaked in silhouette, threatening to reach down and coil her in their branches. But Kerra forged onward, her steps growing more determined. She reached the old corral, bypassed the weather-beaten "No Hunting/No Trespassing" sign, and entered the thickest part of the hollow, her destination clear but her motives uncertain. She swore the sound was increasing in volume with every step. It might as well have been *screaming*. At first it had seemed to echo out of every dark and shadowy corner where she focused her eyes. Then it became steady, continuous, and—thought Kerra—oddly soothing, like the surf of the ocean or the bright melodies of a distant carnival.

All at once every sound was dwarfed by the brush crackling under her feet, the panting in her lungs. She resisted the urge to blink, forcing her eyes wider, afraid she might miss even a fraction of an instant of something important. As a result, her eyes started to tear up, so she wiped them with her sleeve. When she looked again, she realized she had reached the clearing. She stood nearly at its edge. And it was a good thing she'd stopped, because right in front of her gaped a fracture in the earth, a fissure about eight or ten inches wide, running through the woods along a jagged course. Kerra couldn't guess its depth, or how far it extended north or south. It snaked into the undergrowth in either direction, disappearing in the brush. Certainly it wasn't wide enough to swallow her whole, but it could have easily twisted her ankle, perhaps broken her leg. Kerra studied the phenomenon with amazement, then raised her eyes. The pale light and a tall patch of thistles somewhat obstructed her view into the clearing. She again looked at her feet and carefully stepped over the fissure. That single step carried her through the thistles. She raised her eyes again.

And her heart skipped a beat.

She wasn't alone! A person was sitting on the stone where she used to sit—barely twenty feet away! A man, or so she thought. Why hadn't she seen him a second ago? His back was to her. He was wearing some kind of heavy . . . she wasn't sure. The light was still too dim, the shadows too thick. But there was something on his head. A helmet? And several items—tools or something—leaned on the stone beside him. Kerra heard her own startled gasp, the sound of her palm slapping her chest.

The figure leaped to his feet, turning abruptly. He took a defensive stance, reaching toward his belt. *Gracious,* he was arming himself with a *weapon!* He was about to *attack!*

Kerra jolted backwards. The movement was instinctive—and foolish—because she'd forgotten about the crevasse. Her foot dropped out from under her. Her body twisted, and she fell across the fissure. She grunted as her shoulder met the hard earth, but before she could register pain or embarrassment she scrambled back onto one knee, again facing the clearing.

Kerra pulled in her chin in consternation. The man was *gone!*

Now she was thoroughly baffled. Where did he go? She squinted, peering through the thistles. She stood, cutting her eyes to the right and left. The clearing was empty! The man in the leather vest had fled!

Kerra's fear became genuine and feral. Was he circling around to lunge from the bushes? She heard no crackling in the underbrush. It was almost as if he'd *vanished.* But that made no sense. Then again, neither did seeing another human being in these woods at 6:30 in the morning. She looked again in every direction, her heart banging against her ribs.

The man was gone. She half wondered if he'd been there to begin with. Were her senses playing tricks? *No, he'd been there! She wasn't crazy!*

Gritting her teeth, she looked at her feet to make sure she didn't fall in the fissure again, then took a big step across it and raised her eyes.

What happened next transcended all sanity and reason. Kerra thought it resembled the optical effect of staring at a novelty card with a holographic foil image, turning the image slightly, and watching the image shift to a second image. As she crossed the fissure, a shape coalesced from within the thistles—the man in the helmet!—*now less than twelve inches from her face!*

Kerra screamed. But the man was screaming too, his face stretched in shock and surprise. Again, Kerra threw herself backwards. The man seemed to leap back as well, but Kerra didn't stay to confirm it. She scrambled back across the fissure, tearing into the undergrowth, colliding with briars, branches, and leaves. Her grandfather's words passed through her mind—words about strange voices and images.

Kerra felt sure she'd just laid eyes on her first genuine ghost.

CHAPTER

7

KERRA CROUCHED AT THE BASE of a crumbling cement trough with shafts of rebar projecting upward every eight or ten inches. She had made it only as far the old horse corral, certain that she couldn't have made it all the way back to the house before her pursuer caught up. She needed to think, reassess the danger. Her eyes remained glued to the bank of woods between herself and the clearing, certain that the man would soon emerge, perhaps with his weapon in hand, stalking her like a predator.

But the woods had gone still again. Even the Whistlers, or Whisperers, had faded in volume. Kerra cursed herself. Why was she lingering here? What did she hope to see? She should rush back to the house, sound a warning. But what was she supposed to say? *There's a ghost in the hollow! Run for your lives!*

They'd have her committed. She considered having *herself* committed. It was all a mistake. It wasn't real. She'd misinterpreted things somehow. Not the presence of the man—no, the man was *very* real. A young man about nineteen or twenty.

His hair was dark. His eyes, even darker. Perhaps it was just the light. That early-morning dimness was gone now. The day had brightened considerably. The trees, the brush, the shadows—*everything* looked far different than it had only fifteen minutes before. So it seemed safe to believe it was just an optical illusion. What other explanation was there? It was ludicrous to think the man had vanished and reappeared. It was a trick of the light, of the senses. Yes, that was logical. That was sane.

As Kerra recovered herself, she better pieced together the events, as well as the man's appearance. Such a *strange* appearance! He'd worn a uniform of sorts—like the costume of a Roman soldier. But that wasn't it. There were geometric designs on the vest. And feathers on his helmet. An Indian? No, that didn't seem likely. She'd never seen Indians with uniforms like this. And the man's face: definitely not Indian. Then again, some of the features . . . oh, she wasn't sure! It was too dark. Too shadowed. But whatever the case, the man was *real*.

And he was trespassing.

Her nerves settled and calmed. Her powers of reasoning clicked back into place. She remembered that this man had been just as surprised to see *her.* They'd startled each *other.* Perhaps he was hiding like her, somewhere on the other side of the hollow—hiding, not out of fear, but because he'd been *caught.*

But caught doing what? Why was he here? Hunting? This hollow was the home to numerous deer. Perhaps among his weapons there was a compound bow and arrows. Perhaps he was playing a game—a crazy survivalist game like the ones she'd read about where some nutcase goes off into the hills to prove he can subsist for months using only primitive tools, eating roots and berries and such.

Kerra's courage surged anew. In all likelihood, this man was no longer in the vicinity. He'd skedaddled like a jackrabbit, crossed over the hill, and was by now speeding away in his pickup truck, sighing in relief that he'd narrowly avoided a run-in with the property owners—as well as the police, who would have surely arrested him for trespassing, possibly poaching. Suddenly she felt angry. Angry that her spot of privacy had been spoiled.

Feeling an unusual impulse to defend her territory, she started tromping back toward the clearing. But her pace abruptly faltered as she drew near, a much stronger impulse for self-preservation pressing down on her mind. She reached down and filled her grip with an old broken branch. As the fissure in the earth again crossed her path, her movements became tentative. The sunlight was cutting a thousand shafts through the black willow branches, but not in the clearing. No chance of being fooled by illusions now. The clearing looked as bright and clear as at noonday. And it was empty.

Kerra crossed over the fissure, penetrated the last barrier of thistles, and inserted herself into the clearing's center. She lowered the branch. All her feelings of danger and caution ebbed away. She was alone at last.

"*Ka-chuk-a-ti!*"

Kerra's veins turned to ice. The voice had come from her right. She turned sharply, and there he was. The man she had seen only twenty minutes before was standing in a thick cluster of brush. He hadn't fled at all. It was almost as if he'd been *waiting* for her. *Spying!*

But what had he said? She didn't recognize the words. Kerra's legs were frozen in place. So were her lungs. She could neither move nor scream. The stranger in the ancient-looking uniform began walking straight toward her. His broad, muscular body was now protected by a colorful shield. In his right hand was some sort of weapon, long and heavy, with a jagged edge—not of metal, but stone.

He spoke again, but as before, the words were strange— a foreign language, guttural and harsh. But something was happening. The sound was *changing!* Astonishingly, as the man came ever closer, his voice seemed to echo and rever-berate. Or was the reverberation in her own mind? Kerra realized she *did* understand his words. The harsh, guttural syllables transformed into real words—*English* words, as if . . . Kerra had nothing to compare it to. It was only one of a hundred mind-boggling bits of information that her brain was trying to process.

"What are you doing here?" the man demanded sharply. "Don't you realize it's dangerous?" He stopped five paces away, yet continued to glower down, as if with all the intimidation he could muster.

Kerra's fears gave way to another emotion. Indignation would have been a *nice* way to put it. She wanted to tear this guy's head off.

"What am *I* doing here?!" she raged. "This is private property!"

"Property of who? This is wilderness. It's no one's property. Who are you? Where are you from?"

"I'm Corinne and Drew's niece," she shot back. "And if they knew you were here, you'd get a rear end full of buckshot."

"I don't know those names."

"They live right through there. I advise you to get off their property this instant!" Her voice cracked. She feared her anger was buckling—fright was again taking over.

"Right through where?"

Kerra recomposed herself. "I won't ask again. I'll just go back and have them call the police."

The young man was walking around her, maintaining the same distance at every angle. His eyes were moving all over her, drinking in every inch, almost as if he'd never seen . . . well . . . never seen a *woman* before. Kerra continually turned to keep facing him.

"If I scream, they'll hear me. They'll arrive before you can blink an eye." Actually, Kerra wasn't sure of this at all. It was over a hundred yards to the house, and with her voice muffled by all these trees . . .

"Why are you dressed so strangely?" he asked.

Kerra raised her eyebrows. *"Me?* Why am *I—?* Have you looked in a mirror?"

"What is your name?" he demanded. "What is your tribe?"

He'd moved so close that Kerra struck at him with her stick. The man, however, caught it easily. He yanked it from her palm and tossed it away. Kerra raised her hands, palms out—a defensive posture—certain now that she was dealing with a lunatic, maybe an escaped mental patient! "Listen . . . um . . . I'm going home now. I'll just leave you here to do your . . . play your Aztec, Apache—"

He raised his weapon. Kerra's eyes bugged out. Now that she could see it plainly, she concluded it was the gnarliest-looking weapon she'd ever set eyes on—a broad stick with black volcanic glass inset along either edge, like the snout of a sawfish.

"You're not going anywhere," seethed the man. "You're one of them, aren't you?"

"One of . . . *'them'*?" Kerra repeated, her spine rigid.

"A Gadianton! It's just like them to send a woman spy."

A cry crept into her voice. "I-I swear to you—I-I don't know what you're talking about—"

"Then what is your tribe?!" he shouted in her face. *"What is your name?!"*

"S-Sakerra!"

She'd blurted the name, her *original* name, as if it had sprung from a fountain deep inside. Both hands were protecting her face now. She felt woozy, but before she allowed herself to faint, she braved one last glance at her executioner.

To Kerra's surprise, the man's whole countenance had changed, eyes wide with wonder, mouth dangling. Slowly, he lowered his sword. He suddenly looked as vulnerable and timid as Kerra.

"Sakerra?" he repeated. It floated off his tongue, almost with reverence, as if he'd heard this name before. As if . . . he *knew* her.

Kerra slowly took down her hands. She was speechless.

She could only gape at the young man's sharply chiseled face, stare beyond it, through it, and around it, piecing together an image that couldn't possibly be connected with any real memory. A dream, a childhood fairy tale. The image of a magical boy who had once filled her world with every reason she'd ever needed to live.

He removed his helmet, revealing every lock of shining black hair. "It's *me*," he declared, his voice barely louder than a whisper. "It's Kiddoni."

•　•　•

Once again Kerra fled from the clearing, this time shaking her head in disbelief, and with her eyes clouded by tears. He called her name as she ran away, but she didn't turn back. It didn't make sense. It couldn't be true. The branches and leaves rushed past her in a blur, in a fog.

The Donny-Kid. Kid-Donny. Kiddoni.

She hardly remembered the journey to the farmhouse, and it surprised her when she reached her uncle's front porch. As she rushed through the front door, her cousins were gathered in the living room, hair askew, blankets wrapped around their shoulders, having just awakened. Corinne was on the kitchen phone. She looked up as she heard Kerra enter.

"Never mind," she told Grandpa Lee on the other end. "She just showed up." Pulling the phone from her ear, Corinne called, "Kerra?"

But Kerra didn't stop. She ran straight up the stairs, slipped into Natasha's bedroom, and shut the door. Then she pressed into the wall at the far corner of Natasha's bed, her face glistening with tears. She didn't want anyone to see her like this. They would ask her to explain. But how *could* she explain? Everything was still swirling in a cyclone.

A few minutes later she heard a light knock. "Kerra, are you all right?"

She wiped her eyes swiftly and struggled to make her voice sound normal. "Yes, Aunt Corinne. I'll be out in a minute."

"All right," came an eventual, skeptical reply. "Breakfast is ready. Eggs. The earthquake didn't crack a single one."

"I'll be right there," said Kerra.

Her aunt's footsteps retreated. Kerra hugged the pillow tighter to her chest.

The Donny-Kid. Kid-Donny. Kiddoni.

They'd lock her away, just as her mother had always threatened. Kid-Donny was a figment of her imagination. She'd been telling herself this for twelve years. She'd come to believe it. How could he be anything else? That boy. The funny, wonderful little boy. Her imaginary friend. At times she really *was* pretending. Sometimes she would talk to him at night, in the darkness of her bedroom. But that was only in later years—after she didn't see him anymore. After her mother had taken her away from this place forever.

Her tears flowed more heavily. Some were tears of relief. She *wasn't* crazy. The memories were real—memories from when she was four or five years old. Kid-Donny was *real.* The little dark-haired boy who would talk to her for hours, showing her dances, telling her stories of warriors and journeys to faraway lands—*he was real!* Sometimes he would show her magic tricks. He would *disappear!* Then reappear! Sometimes, when they reached out to touch one another, they would feel nothing. Their hands would pass through each other. They played the same game with a beautiful green and blue feather. Kerra would reach out to catch it, but it would fall right through her palm. And yet sometimes—oh, the recollection was so dim!—she was certain that they could feel each other perfectly. He'd held her hand—she was *sure* of it. It was there in her mind—in her memory.

But it was no little boy that she'd seen this morning. It was a man—a warrior. What did it all mean? How was it explained? The Whistlers. The flood of a decade earlier. The earthquake. The fissure in the earth. Maybe she really *was* nuts! The ghost from her childhood was back to haunt her. Back to drive her over the brink!

Get a grip, Kerra told herself. She'd seen *something.* There was no denying it. All at once she felt silly for having fled. He'd *remembered* her! Kerra sprang to her feet. She had to go back a third time. *Now! No time to lose!* But how could she get away? Her aunt was expecting her downstairs. Kerra didn't want to draw suspicion. And she didn't want anyone following her. She wasn't ready to reveal her secret. Not until she understood more. She had to speak with Kiddoni again.

Kerra detoured into the bathroom and washed her face. She rinsed the blood off her forearm—a scratch from a briar. Then she straightened her clothes, drew a deep breath, and went down to breakfast.

The family was gathered around the table, all but Uncle Drew, who was no doubt at work in the orchard. The radio was on in the kitchen—more news of the quake:

" . . . *the only structural damage so far comes from a home in Silver Reef that reported a new crack in the driveway. There are also reports of broken glass, shattered dishes, and objects falling off shelves. But so far no reports of any injuries, just a lot of shaken-up people here in St. George and the surrounding communities from last night's 4.9 earth-shaker centered just outside of Leeds, about fifteen miles north of . . .*"

As Kerra approached the table, Natasha was talking excitedly. "I heard it when I woke up. Why am I always the only one?" Upon seeing Kerra, Natasha immediately set on her. "Kerra, did you hear it? Did you hear the Whistlers?"

"That's enough!" said Aunt Corinne, setting the pitcher of orange juice on the table. "After last night the children are frightened enough without stirring up more of that nonsense."

Brock noted that Kerra looked a little reluctant, perhaps even jittery, as she sat down.

"Where were you?" he asked.

"I . . . went for a walk," Kerra replied.

Aunt Corinne scooped some eggs onto Kerra's plate. "You weren't here when Drew left for work."

"I'm sorry," said Kerra.

"Did you see any cracks in our driveway?" asked Teancum.

"I didn't notice," said Kerra.

Grandpa Lee suddenly entered through the front door. The children greeted him delightedly. Tessa went to give him a hug. "Just wanted to make sure everyone was still in one piece," he said.

"We're fine," said Corinne. "Dad, have you eaten?"

He took a seat beside Kerra. "Don't mind if I do."

Skyler said to his grandfather, "Some geology guys are coming today. They think the epicenter was right in the middle of our hollow. They're gonna survey the whole area."

Kerra stiffened with dread. "How do you know?"

"They called a half hour ago," said Corinne.

That was it. No more procrastination. Kerra started to rise. "I have to go."

Aunt Corinne frowned. "Wait! You haven't touched—"

But Kerra was already headed for the door. She turned around once, still walking backwards. "I'm sorry. I-I'm not hungry. Please, I . . . I'll be back."

She left the house quickly. Brock watched after her with great curiosity.

• • •

Kerra approached the clearing, this time with less fear, but still with an overwhelming sense of uncertainty about what she might see. She reached the fracture along the clearing's edge and thought to herself: *The fissure—this is it. The barrier. The crossing point.*

It was here that the two realities mixed and mingled, like fresh water from the Santa Clara River mixing with the roiling, salty Pacific. Beyond this point, two realities became one. But what reality was *his* reality? How was it defined? Was he from another time? Another universe? Kerra shuddered in exasperation. She'd seen too many sci-fi movies. Most likely he was . . . *what?* There was no starting point even to speculate. Maybe the way it worked in science-fiction movies was dead on.

Carefully, she stepped over the fissure, locking her eyes on the stone in the middle, then taking two more steps to clear the patch of thistles. But the clearing was empty. The man in ancient battle gear was nowhere in sight. Her eyes flashed about, trying to keep it all in focus at once. She took several more steps, as wary as a leopard. Perhaps the barrier was *not* the fissure. Perhaps it was a few yards farther. Exactly how much area did this 'mixing zone' encompass? Ten square feet? A hundred?

She arrived at the stone in the center. Nothing seemed out of the ordinary. Birds chittered away in the branches. Even the *sound* was gone—the Whistlers. The phenomenon seemed to have dissipated with the rising of the sun. This caused her to wonder—was this occurrence only connected with darkness or twilight? Or was it gone for good? Had the breach been mended? Had reality healed its own wound?

Her heart knotted up, and she sat down heavily on the stone. He was gone. Her fantasy from childhood had been reborn, only to fade just as instantly.

"You're back."

She turned sharply. The voice had spoken to her from behind. Kiddoni was standing just this side of the fissure, beyond the thistles. His sword with the volcanic glass was strapped behind his shoulder. His shield had been lowered. He still had his helmet, but it was balanced in the crook of his elbow. Kerra perceived the same vulnerability in his eyes that she'd seen just before she fled back to the house. She stood up, and found that it was still surprisingly difficult to breathe.

Softly, he inquired, "It *is* you, isn't it? Sakerra?"

She nodded.

He smiled—a boyish, delighted smile—utterly out of character with all those harsh-looking weapons and armor.

"You've grown," he said.

"So have you," said Kerra, swallowing.

"I must have visited here a thousand times after . . . after you stopped coming." Suddenly there was a hint of pain in his eyes. "Why? Why did you stop coming?"

"I . . . I couldn't—"

"I chose this as my post—this place in the wilderness. My favorite place in the world. But that was only because of you. Because I hoped someday that you might . . . that I would see you again."

Kerra sat again on the stone. "Wow," she said a little dizzily. It almost sounded like an expletive. She was totally overwhelmed, and she could feel her eyes again start filling with tears.

"Please don't cry," said Kiddoni. "You used to cry all the time when we were little. But I never understood why an angel should cry."

"I stopped believing in you. I *couldn't* believe in you." She looked up at him. "What did you call me?"

He hesitated, then repeated, "An angel."

She cocked her head, surprised.

"That's what you are, isn't it? My father used to think you must be a demon, but I told him no. Only an angel could be so beautiful."

"Don't call me that," said Kerra. "I'm about as much of an angel as Della Reese."

Now it was Kiddoni's turn to look confused.

"Never mind." She looked hard at Kiddoni. All the questions she'd never asked blazed like flashing neon in her mind. Questions that hadn't mattered to a five-year-old girl, but that seemed vitally important now. Her eyes squinted, drawing him into full focus. "What *are* you, Kiddoni?"

He considered the question, then he appeared to stand

a little straighter as he proudly announced, "I'm a Nephite. A descendant of the tribe of Joseph and a descendant of Father Lehi who led our ancestors across the Great Waters. And I'm a warrior in the army of Gidgiddoni. This is my outpost. I watch for enemy spies."

Kerra crinkled her nose. "Enemy spies?"

"Robbers of Gadianton," he clarified, a note of venom in his voice. "They infest all these mountains and forests. My people have gathered their possessions to my homeland of Zarahemla in self-defense."

Her eyes widened. She tried to re-pronounce the word. "Zara-hem—?"

Kiddoni half closed one eye. He suddenly looked suspicious. "If you're not an angel, what are *you?*"

"A girl," she replied. "Just a girl. My land is called America. This—" She raised her arms. "This is *all* America. Utah, to be exact. Over there is a little town called Leeds. And another one called St. George is just—"

He shook his head, almost as if his intelligence were being insulted. "There are no settlements over there." He pointed north. "Zarahemla is *that* way, through the jungles."

She shook her head. "I'm afraid there are no jungles here—not in *my* universe. Mostly, it's desert."

"My *what?*"

"Universe." Kerra realized she was only confusing him. "I don't expect you to understand. I hardly understand myself. Listen, Kiddoni, I think we both live in two universes. Two separate phases of reality."

He still looked completely baffled.

Kerra persisted. "We may occupy the same spot of ground, but . . . but except for this very spot, we never see each other. Does that make sense?"

He shook his head. Kerra sighed in frustration. She plainly needed to sit him down to watch a few episodes of *Star Trek* to bring him up to speed.

Kiddoni erupted and said, "This is—and always *has*

been—the wilderness of Zarahemla. The land of my forefathers. So named for the first man who possessed it, Zarahemla, a descendant of Mulek, son of King Zedekiah of Old Jerusalem, who crossed the Great Waters to escape the great destruction inflicted by Babylon under the brutal hand of—"

Kerra perked up. "What was that?"

Kiddoni paused. "Which part?"

"Old Jerusalem. Babylon. Your people came here from the Middle East? They came from . . . from *Israel?*"

He drew his eyebrows together. "Yes."

Kerra put her hand to her forehead in astonishment. "You're from the *past.*"

He raised an eyebrow. "From *what?*"

"From the past! Don't you see? You're from a land that hasn't existed for . . . I don't know. Maybe thousands of years! Kiddoni, I'm from your *future!*"

He stood there, digesting it all. At last he replied, "This is nonsense."

Kerra became sympathetic. "Hey, I'm sorry. I'm sure this is all way too much for you to take in."

Now he really *was* insulted. "I'm not a dullard. Why am *I* in the past? Maybe *you're* in the past."

She shook her head. "No. I'm very sorry. It's—"

"Why are you so sure?"

"From the things you said. About Old Jerusalem and Babylon . . ." She decided to try another tack. "How long ago did your people cross the ocean?"

"Six hundred years," he answered quickly, as if the swiftness of the answer somehow strengthened his argument.

"Six hundred." She concentrated. "Then that would make it . . ."

He answered for her. "—the sixth month of the nineteenth year since the sign of our Lord's birth. In a few years hence there will be—"

"Wait, wait, wait," said Kerra. "What Lord?"

"Jesus the Messiah, of course."

Kerra's jaw dropped. *"What?"*

"You've never heard of Jesus the Messiah? Then you could *not* be from the future. In the future *everyone* will know of—"

"No, no, I've heard of Jesus Christ," said Kerra. "I just wasn't aware that . . . I didn't know that anyone here had ever—I mean, of *course* people on this continent have known about Jesus since the 1500s when the Spanish came and conquered . . . oh, dear."

Kerra realized what she had done. She'd told a man his destiny. The destiny of his people. She tried to put herself in his position. It occurred to her—even though everybody might *think* they want to know about the future, when it comes right down to it . . .

Kerra continued, "I didn't mean to—"

Unexpectedly, Brock's voice called out from the thick brush, twenty yards behind them. *"Kerra!"*

They turned toward the sound. Kiddoni immediately adopted a defensive stance and drew his weapon from behind his shoulder.

"It's all right," Kerra tried to assure him. "It's my brother."

Kiddoni looked at her, as if judging whether she were telling the truth, then said, "He must keep his voice down, or these entire woods will be swarming with—"

"I'll go to him," said Kerra. "Actually I just came to warn you. People are coming here."

"Gadiantons?"

"Geologists. People from *my* world. They're—never mind. Just stay away from here for a while. A day or two."

"I can't desert my post," said Kiddoni.

"Then hide!" said Kerra in frustration. "Please! If they find you there's no telling—"

Brock called out again. He sounded as if he were stuck. Obviously he'd tried to follow her and gotten trapped in the brambles.

"I have to go," said Kerra. She started to leave the clearing.

"Wait!" snapped Kiddoni. He seemed to have had

enough of this girl's comings and goings. He stepped in front of her to try and prevent her departure. But as Kerra braced herself to collide with Kiddoni's chest, she felt absolutely nothing. Her body ran *right through him!* She passed through the Nephite as if he were Casper the Friendly Ghost! She spun back and saw him still standing there. They gaped at each other, mystified. Finally, Kerra turned away. She left him there and continued toward the sound of her brother's voice.

She found him a moment later. As she'd guessed, he'd gotten himself into a nest of brush and brambles.

"You can't get through that way!" she called to him. "Go back!"

"I'm *stuck*," he growled. "Who were you talking to?"

"No one. Stay there. I'm coming around."

After rescuing him, Kerra insisted that they return to the farmhouse. She continued to play innocent, but Brock wasn't having any of it.

"I know what I heard," he said.

"No, you *don't*," said Kerra stubbornly.

They were still discussing the matter a few hours later as several white trucks filled with geologists and other state employees parked along their driveway. Sherilyn had overheard Brock's accusations and Kerra's denials. Her imagination filled in the rest. As they stood at the living room window and watched the trucks arrive, she asked Kerra, "Did you really see someone? One of Grandpa's ghosts?"

"NO!" Kerra blurted out. "There was NO ONE! Chill out! *Everybody!*"

She'd had quite enough of all of them. Kerra made another exit, leaving the house for the third time that day. She passed the three white trucks. The geologists looked up from their clipboards and transit instruments. One even whistled a catcall, but Kerra was not distracted from her objective.

It was time to ask her grandfather some pointed questions.

8

S HE LEANED OVER THE DESK, cradling her chin in her hands, as Grandpa Lee lovingly carved the neck of his next violin, sliding the scraper away from him and leaving a residue of little wood curls.

"Grandpa," asked Kerra, "what's a Nephite?"

The question earned his immediate attention. "A Nephite is a descendant of Nephi. It's the name of a group of people who once lived in ancient America. Did you hear that word at church?"

"No," said Kerra, but as her grandfather raised an eyebrow, she changed her answer. "I mean, yes. That's right. I heard it at church."

"The Nephites were once a powerful nation. They built cities, ships, temples. Their civilization lasted more than a thousand years."

"What happened to them?"

He started carving again and said solemnly, "They were destroyed."

"By who?"

"By the Lamanites—descendants of Laman. You see, Nephi and Laman were brothers. They crossed the ocean around 600 B.C. Then, after the death of their father, Lehi, their two tribes became bitter enemies. The feud was carried on by their children, and by their children's children, for many centuries."

"Where did they live?"

"Where? We're not quite sure. Somewhere in this hemisphere. Most seem to think it was in Central or South America."

"Not here?"

"You mean in Utah? Maybe some lived here. We don't know for sure."

"Were there ever jungles here?"

He chuckled. "Maybe sixty-five million years ago."

Kerra bit her lip. It still didn't make sense. Apparently this phenomenon wasn't just a rift in time, but a rift in *geography*. Frustrated, she said, "Why haven't I heard of these tribes?"

"I guess you gotta be a Mormon."

"How do Mormons know?"

He stopped working again, hesitated a moment, then seemed to make a decision. He went over to a shelf filled with dusty books and pulled one off—a beautiful old volume with brown, beaded leather. He set it down right in front of her. The gold embossing practically jumped off the cover: *The Book of Mormon.*

"General Authority Edition, 1888," he said. "First one they ever broke down into chapters and verses. Francis M. Lyman of the Quorum of the Seventy was its first owner. His signature is right there on the inside flap. If you're careful, you're welcome to read it. I mean, if you'd like to."

She stared at it uneasily at first. Then with one eye half shut, she asked, "Are you trying to convert me, Grandpa?"

In the movie, the hunters from Chapter 1 shoot an elk, not a deer. (No animals were hurt.) This sequence was filmed on location at LC Ranch near Altamont, Utah. Right to Left, Leonard Surprise (Beaumont), Chris Heimerdinger (The Hunter), and Dave Walker (Clacker).

The Hunter (Chris Heimerdinger) makes his way through the foggy woods in pursuit of the wounded elk. Moments later, the tremor will strike.

The blood on the Hunter's cheek is not his own, but from the elk. From Chapter 1: *"He collapsed to his knees. He'd been shot! His focus fell on the shaft of an arrow, protruding from his right shoulder. The feathers were blue and exotic, the wood banded by colorful designs, like something from another age. He reached back and felt the arrowhead sticking out behind his shoulder, so sharp it cut his finger. Panic avalanched through his soul."*

From Chapter 1: *"The shadows from the woods were descending on him like wolves. His uninjured arm flew up to shield his face. The Hunter screamed."*

The "hollow" near Leeds, Utah. This photograph is looking north. The McConnell's farmhouse can be seen in the midst of the woods. Lee Instruments violin shop is the smaller building toward the top and far left of the page. The strip of woods continues a little farther north and considerably farther south.

The McConnell's farmhouse, as seen from the bluff just to the northeast. Clearly seen is the wrap-around porch, van, and the garage where Skyler McConnell repairs his jalopies.

Kevin Lee, the real violin maker on whom the character of Grandpa Lee McConnell is based. Kevin is a longtime friend of the author, and also an author in his own right, having penned *The Two Trees* and other books in the "Luthier Diaries" series. He stands in the midst of the unusual, twisted woods of the hollow.

This is the interior of Lee Instruments, Kevin Lee's violin shop, located near Leeds, Utah. The wood above Kevin's head will become the fronts, backs, necks, etc., of future violins. This wood is from all over the world, and some of it has been "curing" for more than a decade.

He slapped his chest, as if wounded. "No! Of course not! I wouldn't . . . Well, yes. Yes, I am. A little."

Kerra grinned. Then she leaned over and kissed him on the cheek.

• • •

Kerra leafed through the Book of Mormon as she ambled home down the long driveway. When at last she looked up, she noticed that the geologists' white pickups were gone. *Finally,* she thought. She looked both ways, then descended into the woods.

The shadows were long. Everything—the trees, the ground, and the distant hills—seemed to have a glowing sheen of bullion gold. She arrived at the clearing, but Kiddoni was nowhere present. Her heart sank. It actually surprised her how *low* it sank, and how frightened she became. What if Kiddoni had faded away again? If the miracle that had made him appear was truly some sort of disturbance—some sort of rift in time and space—obviously it was just as fragile now as it had been when she was a little girl. The phenomenon might have already corrected itself. A chill rushed through her soul.

But as she crossed the fissure, something unusual caught her eye at the base of the stone in the center. There, stuck in the ground, was a stunning blue and green feather. She could only imagine the exotic bird it might have come from—certainly not one from southern Utah. Kerra reached down and plucked it from the earth. She realized immediately that it was the same kind of feather that she remembered from twelve years earlier—the same feather that she and Kiddoni had played a game with as children.

Anxiously, Kerra looked about. He'd left it for her—she knew it. But where was he now? Then Kerra spotted another feather at the far edge of the clearing. She approached, but just as she joined it in her hand with the first feather, she spotted a *third* feather. A trail?

Kerra retrieved a fourth feather a few yards farther on. As she looked back she realized she was now some distance from the clearing—at least two dozen yards. She turned to continue on the trail, and something new captured her eye. Balanced in the crook of a black willow branch was a small bundle of flowers. The colors were extraordinary—exotic and tropical. Kerra went to it, but as she reached out to take the bundle, another hand reached out from behind the tree and gently snatched her fingers in midflight. It was Kiddoni.

Kerra gasped in fright, causing the Nephite to blush with guilt.

"I'm sorry," he said. "I shouldn't have startled you."

But it wasn't Kiddoni's appearance that had startled Kerra. She gawked in wonder as Kiddoni's strong hand grasped her own.

"I can *feel* you!" she exclaimed. "I don't understand."

"It's like before," said Kiddoni, referring again to their encounter in childhood. "Sometimes I could touch you, and sometimes . . ."

"The rift must be widening," said Kerra. "It's becoming stronger."

With that Kiddoni's expression changed. He looked sullen as he released her hand. "I believe you now."

"Believe what?"

"That you come from the future while I . . . while I'm a man of the past. I spoke briefly with my Chief Captain, Gidgiddoni. He confirmed what you said about the destiny of the Nephites. In fact, it's been taught by the prophets since the days of Lehi. Everything I do now—the causes I fight for—will make no difference in the end. My people, my cities—they will all be destroyed."

"But that may not be for hundreds of years," said Kerra.

"So what happens between now and then? Is there

anything to look forward to? Or will I have to watch as my people are slowly crushed, like corn under a grinding stone, until there's nothing left?"

Kerra scoffed. "Now you're just feeling sorry for yourself. I'm sure there's a lot to look forward—"

"What is that?" He referred to the antique volume in her hands.

"Oh," said Kerra, almost forgetting she had it. "It's a book. About you, I think. Your people. A history."

"Did you bring that here to gloat?"

"Now stop that," she said, as if scolding a pouting child. "Actually, I haven't read it yet."

Intrigued, Kiddoni reached out. "Let me see it."

Kerra handed it over.

He opened it, but then he seemed quite annoyed. "I can't read this! What language is it?"

"The same one you're speaking," said Kerra.

"I speak the language of my forefathers. The language of the Hebrews. What do you think you're speaking?"

"English."

"Do you think I'm a fool? Don't you think I'd know my own language—?"

"Stop it!" Kerra snapped. "Can you stop barking like a walrus long enough to think? It's part of the miracle. That's what this is, you know. A miracle."

"Walrus?" he asked unexpectedly.

"It's a large—never mind. My point is—"

But Kiddoni's mood abruptly changed again. He put a finger to his lips to silence her. "Shhh! Come with me."

He took Kerra's hand one more time and led her up the hillside behind them. Kerra struggled to keep from dropping the book, as well to hang on to all of her feathers and flowers. After a few minutes they reached a stone shelf overlooking the hollow from the west. Right away Kiddoni pointed toward the roof of a house clearly poking up from the midst of the trees. "Now you can tell me. Whose palace is that?"

The sight sent a shock up Kerra's spine. "Holy—!" She yanked on Kiddoni's arm and forced him to duck. "They can see us! Keep down!"

"It wasn't there yesterday," said Kiddoni.

"It's my aunt and uncle's farmhouse. Like I told you—the rift is widening."

Kiddoni narrowed his gaze and said analytically, "I've been debating whether or not I should attack it."

"Please don't," said Kerra.

"But it's right in the path of the invasion!"

Kerra pulled in her chin. "*Excuse me?*"

Kiddoni arose and walked away a few steps, sighing in futility. "Never mind. No one believes me anyway."

She wasn't about to let that go. She came to her feet and joined him. "What do you mean 'invasion'?"

"The Gadianton army. If they attack, their warriors could march right through here."

"Gadiantons?" asked Kerra. That wasn't a word her grandfather hadn't mentioned. "Don't you mean . . . Lamanites?"

"Some Gadiantons are Lamanites," said Kiddoni. "Some Nephites, too. Gadiantons are a secret society of sorcerers, plunderers, and murderers. They infest all these mountains. For years they infiltrated our cities—Nephite *and* Lamanite— corrupting our leaders, binding their members with bloody oaths, murdering those who believed in the coming Messiah. My people were forced to gather into one place for their own protection. Someday the Gadiantons will attack. It's inevitable. You see, we left our fields desolate. They're too lazy to do honest work, so they're starving. Lachoneus thinks they won't come for another season, but my assignment is still important."

He felt an instrument on his belt, some kind of horn with

symmetrical designs, perhaps for warning others. Then his hand moved to the black-bladed weapon behind his shoulder. His eyes scanned the hollow. "Some would say this is not the most important watchpost." He drew the sword. "But it doesn't matter. I'll stay alert. I hate them all. They murdered my father. A Gadianton killed my oldest brother. This time, I'll be ready."

He took several artful swipes at the air. Kerra winced, but at the same time, she was substantially impressed.

Kiddoni peered keenly into the trees, like a lion searching for prey. "Honestly, I think this place is *quite* strategic. If I was old Giddianhi—"

"Giddianhi?"

"Their villainous leader." He continued. "If I was old Giddianhi, I'd send my army creeping right through this ravine, under the cover of these trees. The woods are thick. Full of briars. But that's what makes it the most advantageous—the most unexpected. Yes, I think they underestimated this spot." He turned to Kerra. "You agree?"

She was so entranced watching his actions that the question jarred her. She gave a little shrug and shook her head. Kiddoni was staring at her as well. He suddenly acted a bit self-conscious.

Kerra indicated the sagebrush plains to the east, dotted here and there with a few modular homes. "Kiddoni, what do you see when you look over there? Do you see the houses? Do you see my uncle's almond orchards?"

"I see the hills of Gideon," said Kiddoni. "The wilderness of Hermounts."

Kerra pointed west. A glowing sunset was presently illuminating the long I-15 Freeway and the sleepy town of Leeds. "And over there?"

Kiddoni took a few steps toward the region she indicated. "Forests and jungles. Beyond is the city of Zarahemla."

Kerra's eyes suddenly widened. Kiddoni was *fading!* She

could actually perceive the glow of the orange sun through his torso and head.

"Stop!" she gasped.

Kiddoni turned.

Kerra stepped toward him. "You're there! You're at the edge of the rift!"

Panicking, she reached out to pull him back. But as she tried to grasp his bronze-colored forearm, her hand passed right through the flesh. Kerra stumbled backwards. The Nephite's reaction was instinctive and lightning swift. He lunged toward her to stop the fall. The next thing Kerra realized, she was in his arms. He'd come back into perfect focus. She embraced him with relief.

"It must take in most of the hollow now—all along the fault line," she said breathlessly. "Let's go back."

They descended back into the woods. He held her hand most of the way. As they neared the clearing, he said, "You must tell me of your people. Have they built many cities? Are your numbers great?"

Kerra blew the air from her cheeks. "More than I could ever count. There are millions and millions. And some cities are so big it would take you days to walk from one end to the other."

Kiddoni was astonished. "Your people must be very powerful."

"I guess so," said Kerra. "In some ways. But in most ways I think we're no different from you."

"Are there any more wars? I was told that when the Messiah comes, there will be no more fighting. Only peace."

"Oh, there's still plenty of wars and fighting," said Kerra. "I guess the peace doesn't come until later."

They arrived at the clearing. Kerra sat upon the stone.

"That is unfortunate," said Kiddoni solemnly. "All my life, all I've known is war and turmoil. Our people have always had many enemies. My father used to say it was only by the grace of God that we have survived as long as we have."

"He sounds like he was a wise man."

His expression saddened. "He listened to the prophets. My mother too, before she died. And she listened to her heart. Perhaps I'll marry a girl like her someday." He assessed Kerra again. "What about you?"

"What?"

"Are you betrothed?"

"Heavens! I'm seventeen years old!"

"Is there something wrong with you?"

She pulled a face and huffed, "Of course not! What do you mean?"

"Well, I—I'm just surprised."

Kerra let go of his hand and walked just ahead. "I don't want to get married. I'm not sure I believe in it. I've never seen it bring anything but misery."

"You don't want to marry? *Ever?*" asked Kiddoni.

She could see that this disturbed him greatly, and tried to dismiss the subject by saying, "Okay, maybe when I'm forty."

Kiddoni was only further incensed. "*Forty!* A woman's child bearing years are past!"

Kerra huffed. "That's perfectly fine with me."

"What is life without a husband and family?"

"Like heaven," Kerra replied smugly. "I want to live my life doing what I want. Your women might be perfectly happy having babies, cooking, and lugging water all day. But here . . ."

"We cherish our women," countered Kiddoni, "like so many birds of paradise. A good husband takes his wife into his heart, and they are one for all time and eternity."

Kerra sucked in her cheek, realizing she'd probably pushed this too far. "I didn't mean to offend you," she said sincerely.

"I think," Kiddoni leaned closer, "you just don't know what it feels like."

"What *what* feels like?"

"To be really loved."

She opened her mouth to protest, but nothing came out.

Kiddoni continued, "You—*every* woman—should be loved so deeply that nothing else matters. Not war, or upheaval, or . . . lugging water. It should sustain you, and the feeling should only grow stronger."

He'd said it looking straight into her soul, not batting an eye.

Kerra squirmed a little. "Well, that's fine for some, I guess." Her face felt flush. She wanted to shake her head at him, brush it all off with a laugh. But she couldn't do it. *He really is a fantasy,* she thought. Something outside the bounds of reality.

Instead, she gave a coy smile. "You're pretty good at this."

"What's that?"

"Charming the socks off a girl."

He shrugged, "I speak from the heart." He shut one eye at her. "Socks?"

Kerra laughed. But before she realized it, Kiddoni's mind again seemed to venture to another world. He stared straight ahead. Again, the Nephite's expression went as hard as granite and his mood did a sudden turnabout.

"Perhaps you're right," he said soberly. "Such sentiments may not be for everyone. They are not for me. Only for those who know peace. I cannot think of such things. Not yet. Perhaps not ever. First I will avenge my family's blood. I will kill as many of them as I can, even—if necessary—to my dying breath."

She studied him for a long moment. "It can't be good," she began finally. "I mean, I don't think it could *ever* be good to feel so much hate."

The statement seemed to irritate him. "Hate is all I have right now."

"But you can't change things," said Kerra. "You can't change what happened. Maybe you should let it go."

He bristled. "Those are the words of a coward. I *will* change things. I will fight for my people."

"That's not what I mean. I mean . . . wow. I'm sorry. It's just . . . nothing lasts, Kiddoni. Especially things you love. You can count on it."

Kiddoni's face softened. "Do you believe in nothing?"

"Not really," Kerra shrugged. "Not much."

She could feel tension building inside. Finally she leaped to her feet. "*Ahhh!* This is all so crazy! It isn't right. It's not real. *You're* not real. *Everything*—this miracle—it could all go away at any instant, and I'd never see you again."

Kiddoni reached out one more time to take her hand. "But it's here now. *We're* here."

Kerra pulled away. "I have to go. They'll start looking."

She tucked the Book of Mormon and the flowers under her arm and began walking toward the edge of the clearing.

"But you'll be back. Yes?" Kiddoni asked in earnest.

She paused just before crossing the fissure in the earth, and faced him once more. "Maybe . . . Yes."

"You see?" said Kiddoni, his grin slightly twisted. "You still have some faith, then."

She smiled, unable to help it. Then Kerra continued on, at last becoming hidden by the branches and fronds of the hollow.

• • •

Brock McConnell felt sure that he'd died and gone to the place of fire and brimstone. He was doing his best to make the most of this adventure in the sticks of Utah, but his longing for the night life and excitement of his neighborhood back in California was growing more intense by the hour.

His cousin Teancum was just about as square as a kid could possibly be. He understood *nothing* of what was cool, what was 'in,' or what was fun. The dude collected rocks, for pity's sake! *Rocks!* His second favorite pastime was hunting lizards and tarantulas. The poor kid just wasn't normal. Or maybe it was just that he didn't know any better. If he got the chance, Brock was determined to open up Teancum's sheltered mind to life's more intriguing possibilities.

Brock at least managed to convince him to go to the movies. Corinne dropped the two of them off at the Stadium 8 in St. George. He and Teancum walked along the row of movie posters on the outside wall to decide which one looked best.

"This?" asked Teancum.

They were staring up at a poster with goofy-looking animated pirates.

Brock shook his head. *Was he serious?* "It's a cartoon!"

"But it's cool!" said Teancum.

"You mean you've already seen it?"

"Twice. Once with my sisters, and once with my Sunday School class."

"And you're willing to endure the agony *again?*"

"Sure, if—"

"Oh, man!" Another poster caught Brock's attention. It was an action flick with fire, guns, and beautiful women in black leather. "Yes! Yes! I've been *waiting* for this one!"

Teancum noted the letter printed at the bottom of the poster. "It's rated R."

"So what?" said Brock. "We buy a ticket for something else, then 'accidentally' go into the wrong theater."

"Nah," said Teancum. "If my mom found out, I'd be toast."

Brock gawked at him, then made a growl and moved on

to the next poster—a comedy with another of his favorite actors holding a handful of money and smoking a massive cigar. "Fine," he pouted. "Let's just go to this."

Again Teancum noted the rating. "It's PG-13."

"Huh???"

"I'm not thirteen."

Now Brock was utterly dumbfounded. "You have *got* to be kidding."

Teancum added, "Mom says for some movies like that, I'll *never* be thirteen."

Brock spun around in exasperation. "That's child abuse! *Man!* Just forget it!" Pouting, he plopped himself down on the curb. "How long till your mom comes and gets us?"

Teancum looked at his watch. "Two hours. Unless I call her to come back." He sat on the curb beside his exasperated cousin. He was feeling a little exasperated himself. "What do you wanna do?"

Brock raised his eyes and gazed out across the theater's darkened parking lot. Slowly, a grin climbed the boy's cheeks. He gave Teancum a sideways glance, then urged him to follow with a subtle nod of the head.

Brock led Teancum through the rows of various vehicles, almost as if he were walking down the aisle of a toy store.

"What do you like?" asked Brock.

"You mean cars?"

Brock gave him a strange look. "No, tricycles. Of *course* cars!"

With that, Teancum's gaze came to rest on a cherry red Corvette—an older model from the mid-'70s, but gussied up and repainted for the new generation. "Rad!" said Teancum. "My brother would go *nuts* for this."

Brock stopped walking. He glanced about to make sure that no one was watching them, then pulled a strange instrument out from inside his jacket. It looked a little like a pocketknife, but Brock unfolded it like a ruler. There was a hook on one end.

"Teancum, meet my buddy, Mr. Slim-Jim."

Teancum watched, his face registering dismay, as Brock slipped the tool down between the window and the door on the driver's side of the Corvette. They heard a click—slick as a whistle.

"What are you doing?" Teancum demanded.

Casually, Brock opened the door and revealed the interior to Teancum like a chauffeur to a millionaire. "You wanna see how it handles?"

Teancum clearly couldn't believe what he'd just seen. "You're crazy."

"As a fox," said Brock. "Come on!"

But Teancum turned around and stomped back toward the movie theater. Brock watched for a second, mouth dangling. Finally, he slammed the Corvette's door.

"Unbelievable," he said to himself, and followed after his hayseed cousin.

This was it—that was the straw. Teancum was outa here. Whatever else happened, he was determined that this would be his very last night in the la-la land of Utah.

9

T HE SHADOW MOVED THROUGH the darkness with infinite patience, like a panther on the scent of something wounded, something dying. He knew how to move, how to creep, with the least resistance from his environment, making hardly a sound. Just a scant breath moving over the leaves and through the branches of the forest. There was no light except the moon, but the Shadow needed nothing more. *Wanted* nothing more. It was essential that he remain undetected, invisible to all wary eyes. His mission depended upon this, and failure meant the harshest punishments. Even death.

The going had been steady and uneventful. He'd made this journey once before. He'd returned to verify his first report—that only one lookout had been posted in these woods. His orders were to confirm his enemy's behavior, verify that it was consistent and predictable. This would make it much easier to strike when the time came. They would brush this adversary aside like an irritating gnat, then move on to far greater conquests.

The Shadow knew that he still had some distance to go—at least another three or four minutes through the thickest part of the brush. But all at once something unexpected caught his eye.

What was this?

It was a light. It pierced through the foliage on his right, a strange white light, brighter than any he had ever encountered. It forced the Shadow to alter his course. A light like this had to be investigated.

A short distance farther he stepped out from the final barrier of foliage. The vision unfolded before him. He lingered there in awe. *What in the name of the gods?* It was a building! A large building and . . . it was awash in mystic lights!

But where had it come from? The Shadow had been here only four days ago, and there had been nothing here then. Nothing even remotely like this. Was it possible that he had wandered so far off course? It was the only explanation. He would be punished for this. It would alter the schedule, set things back several days. Perhaps call for an entirely new plan.

But at the moment the vision held him spellbound. He could see into the building. There were windows covered by a substance as transparent as water or air. He could see figures moving around inside, unaware, unexpecting. The Shadow moved steadily closer, his heart pounding like a drum.

The more he saw, the more mesmerizing it all became. There were so many inexplicable things all about him—large objects with wheels, mind-bending sculptures of metal and wood. A strange, vulgar music emanated from inside a smaller building positioned just south of the larger one. He could also hear an awful grinding sound. The Shadow opted to approach this smaller building first. As he reached the wall, he crept around the edge, pressing his back against the surface, until he could see around the corner.

The interior of the smaller building was entirely open to

his view. The Shadow paused to take it in. So many objects of iron and copper. So many things he did not understand. And in the center was a boy. The boy was alone. He was only a few years younger than the enemy the Shadow had come here to find. He was leaning over one of the large wheeled objects, gaping at what appeared to be its internal organs. The grinding, suctioning noise was created by a small object in the boy's hands, a tool of some sort, or a weapon. He used this object to manipulate these internal organs, like a blacksmith at the bellows, or a diviner poised over a sacrificial offering.

The boy didn't see him, and because of it, the Shadow felt powerful. This young one may have been surrounded by a multitude of strange and evil things, nevertheless he looked weak, almost helpless.

He must be dealt with, thought the Shadow. *He must be eliminated before I continue on.*

The Shadow reached for his knife.

• • •

Brock McConnell again glanced out into the hall. He'd made it into his aunt and uncle's bedroom without being seen. It was the only place in the house with a private phone. The rest of the family was gathered in the living room. His sister was upstairs tonight, reading from some book that their grandfather had given her. Brock realized this might be his only chance.

He quickly dialed the number and held the receiver to his ear. After a single ring, there was an answer.

"Hello?" said a low voice.

Brock didn't recognize the voice. He said, as loudly as he dared, his eyes still peeled toward the hallway, "I need to talk to Spree."

"He's not here. He asked me to take his messages."

Brock heard movement outside the room. He said urgently, "It's Brock. He'll know who I am. Tell him . . . tell him to come and get me."

There was a pause on the other end, and then the voice said steadily, "Where are you?"

To Brock's relief, whoever had approached the bedroom had gone into the bathroom one door up the hall.

"I'll give you directions," said Brock into the phone. "Ready?"

• • •

Skyler switched off the air wrench and looked over his work. The engine of his cousin's Pontiac was worse than he'd first suspected. Definitely more than just the alternator. Something to do with the transmission. It looked like he was going to have to break the news to her that it really wasn't worth repairing. Might be cheaper just to purchase a new set of wheels. But he wasn't ready to give up just yet. He reached for the wrench and prepared to get back to work.

That was when he heard the noise. It came from outside the garage, just on the other side of the south wall—a scrape or a bump, like someone knocking against the siding.

"Anyone there?" Skyler called out.

There was no reply. He might have ignored it, decided it was only a cat or a coon and gone back to work, but it just didn't sound like an animal. Oddly, he had a strange feeling that whatever it was, it was still there, almost as if he could hear somebody breathing. Anyway, it was worth taking a look. If one of his sisters was trying to scare him, he'd get the last laugh by scaring her first.

He set down his tools and walked across the floor of the garage, toward the south wall. He was just inches away, prepared to leap out and frighten the frightener, when he heard the creak of the side door of the house.

His mother called out, her tone demanding immediate attention. "Skyler! Do you have any of my good dish towels out there?"

Skyler forgot all about the unusual noise. Nothing frightened him more than his mother's ire—especially when he was guilty as charged. He glanced at some greasy towels on the hood of his Mustang. "The rooster ones?" he asked sheepishly.

"Yes!" Corinne snapped.

"Those are your good ones?"

"Get those in here!" she ordered. "I want them in the washer NOW! With bleach!"

Skyler quickly retrieved the towels and headed toward the house.

• • •

The Shadow leaned out from behind the wall in time to see the boy follow the older woman inside the larger building. This made the Shadow curse under his breath. His opportunity for an easy kill had slipped away.

He moved on, using the wheeled objects to conceal himself, and drew closer to the windows of the main building. He could clearly see a middle-aged man seated upon some furniture with several small children, all gaping into the face of some unseen thing that projected flashes and sparks of colored light. The colors bathed the entire room in an unseemly glow. And yet these people, too, appeared helpless. The Shadow had an instinct about such things. Despite all that seemed mysterious and unexplainable, he felt certain that there was no real threat here. No insurmountable danger to his comrades.

He desired only one further indulgence—just a quick peek into one of the smaller windows where he heard running water, and where something flitted in and out of the light. He moved down the wall and drew closer to the window frame until his nose could almost touch the transparent pane. There was a girl inside. A young girl gazing at her own reflection in a peculiar, flat mirror—a mirror as clear as the stillest pool. The Shadow couldn't dispel his sense of awe and wonder. He stood there a long time—far longer than he had planned. But then the girl's eyes turned. And went as wide as full moons.

There was a bloodcurdling scream.

• • •

Kerra was reading Second Nephi, Chapter 26, verse 22: *"And there are also secret combinations, even as in times of old, according to the combinations of the devil, for he is the founder of all these things; yea, the founder of murder, and works of darkness . . ."*

That was when she heard the scream.

It was such a primal, gut-wrenching scream that it made her sit bolt upright. The voice was Tessa's. Urgently, she rushed to the bottom of the stairs, where she found most of the family gathered in the front room. Seven-year-old Tessa was in her mother's arms, still hysterical. Aunt Corinne was trying to comfort her, pleading to know what had frightened her out of her wits. But she was too distraught to speak and just kept pointing frantically toward the bathroom. Uncle Drew, Teancum, and Brock had already gone down the hall to investigate.

"Tessa! What is it?" pleaded Corinne. "Tell us what's wrong!"

"A man!" screeched Tessa. "In the w-w-window! He w-was—!"

"A man? Who? What did he look like?"

Uncle Drew and the boys returned.

"There's nobody," said Teancum.

"I saw him!" Tessa insisted. "He-he-*ohhh!* All red! He was *horrible!*"

It was several minutes before her nerves had settled enough to describe it. In the meantime, the men gathered flashlights and circled the property. They shined their beams into the thick underbrush of the hollow, though no one was quite willing to venture within. Skyler mentioned that he might have heard something earlier; otherwise there was no evidence that anything unusual had been in the vicinity.

Tessa, still sobbing, finally said, "It was a man. A *bald* man, but there was something on his head—like a skull. He was standing in the window. His face and chest had red designs. He was just *staring* at me!"

"A skull on his head?" asked Natasha.

"Face and chest painted red?" asked Teancum.

"Like blood," Tessa clarified.

Sherilyn scoffed. "Goodness gracious."

"I saw it!" Tessa defended. "I really saw it!"

"Are you sure you weren't sleepwalking and had a nightmare?" Colter suggested.

Corinne came to her daughter's defense. "I believe she saw *something.* But it must have gone away."

"Maybe it was an alien," said Brock sarcastically.

"It was a demon!" said Tessa. "A *monster!*"

"Oh, honey," soothed Corinne. "There's no such thing. *Please* try to remember exactly what you saw."

But the little girl's story didn't change. Most of the children did their best to dismiss it, though several felt inclined to tell ghost stories and scare each other for the rest of the evening. That is, until Corinne broke up the party and sent everyone to bed. Tessa wouldn't sleep anywhere but her parents' bedroom.

Kerra could hardly sleep at all, her imagination spinning. Unlike the others, she believed every word that Tessa had said.

CHAPTER

10

AS SOON AS THE DAWN reared its head, Kerra slipped out the front door and descended into the hollow. She made her way swiftly through the forest. The Whistlers were humming as loudly as ever, although the tone seemed to have changed. It seemed more *even* now, more . . . stable. She bypassed the old horse corral, sailed through the thickest part of the foliage, and approached the clearing.

Even before she crossed over the fissure in the earth, she saw Kiddoni standing there. The warrior was facing her, standing tall, the glow of the dawn illuminating his features. It was almost as if he'd been standing there all night long—perhaps since the moment they'd parted the day before, patiently waiting, as if his life had ended the instant she left and reawakened the moment she drew near. Kerra hesitated for a fraction of a second. She wasn't sure why. Just the sight of him stirred all her senses—emotions that she couldn't even define. Certainly they were feelings that she'd never felt before. She sighed deeply, tried to focus again on the main object of her visit, and continued forward.

Kiddoni perceived almost immediately that something was wrong.

"Are you all right?" he asked.

"Kiddoni," Kerra began, "you spoke yesterday of evil people called Gadiantons. What do they look like?"

Kiddoni's grip tightened on the sword. "Why? Have you seen some?"

"No," said Kerra, trying to keep him from overreacting. "I mean, I don't know. One of my cousins claims she . . . The girl is quite young. She might not have seen *anything,* but—"

"What did she see?"

"These Gadiantons—are they bald? Do they paint themselves red? Do they wear skulls on their heads?"

"A scout!" Kiddoni confirmed. "A Gadianton spy! Where did your cousin see this man?"

"It was last night. Just a hundred and fifty yards from here—back at the farmhouse. She said that she saw him looking in at her through the window."

Kiddoni began pacing, his thoughts swirling rapidly. "I knew it. They're surveying this valley. It's further proof that I've been right. The attack will come from the mountains, right through these woods. They *have* to listen to me now."

"You're the only Nephite guarding this entire valley?" asked Kerra.

"Of course not," said Kiddoni. "There are others. I can signal them with this." He indicated the instrument on his belt that looked like some kind of horn or bugle. "But I'm the only one who felt it was worthwhile to station himself in this ravine. I must warn my captain." He moved as if to leave the clearing.

"Kiddoni, wait!" said Kerra. "Exactly when is this invasion supposed to take place?"

"It could come any day. Any hour." Kiddoni finally saw the serious concern in Kerra's eyes. He stepped toward her and placed his powerful hands on the curve of her shoulders. "Sakerra, you must warn your family." He yanked the horn off his belt. "If there's trouble, blow this with all your strength. The lookout on the next ridge will hear it and sound another warning. Then another warning will sound until the entire Nephite army is alerted. I won't be gone long."

He placed the strange-looking bugle in her hands. Kerra looked down at it, then up into Kiddoni's eyes. Once again the warrior turned to leave. But almost as an afterthought, he paused one last time. Kerra could feel herself starting to tremble, tears pricking at her eyes. But was it caused by fear, or was it the pain of seeing him leave again so soon after their morning reunion?

Something in Kerra's gaze held Kiddoni, and he couldn't quite break away. Almost before Kerra realized it, before she could fully relish it, the warrior took her into his arms. She closed her eyes, and an instant later, she felt his lips pressing into hers. The Nephite kissed her deeply. However, when it ended, it seemed so sudden. Kerra opened her eyes to find him still holding her gaze, drinking her in, as if memorizing every feature and nuance of her countenance. The intensity almost frightened Kerra, and it sent another stab of pain through her heart. She sensed that he too was wondering if they would ever see each other again, and that was almost too much for her to bear. So much so that when he finally released her, there was a kind of sting to it, like tearing tape away from the skin.

"I will return," he promised, sounding more like he was trying to reassure himself.

With that, Kiddoni turned and slipped into the woods. Kerra stood alone in the center of the clearing, her thoughts jumbled and her emotions in a whirlwind. She had to do something. She couldn't just sit around and wait. The secret had finally become too heavy to bear alone.

"Grandpa Lee," she whispered.

Bracing herself, Kerra departed the clearing, walking in the direction of her grandfather's shop.

She was going to tell him everything.

•   •   •

As soon as Kerra exited the clearing, Brock emerged from the brush. His eyes were looking toward the woods where Kerra had disappeared, but his steps were following Kiddoni. He'd seen and heard *everything* from his hiding place in the trees. This time in following his sister he'd been far more careful, and his stealth had most definitely paid off. His eleven-year-old mind still wasn't sure what to make of it all. But whatever it meant—whoever this man in the Indian costume really was—it could certainly prove more interesting to follow him than Kerra. Again Brock looked after his sister to make sure she wasn't going to return. Then he started swiftly down the trail cut by the man his sister had called a "Nephite."

It wasn't long before he caught sight of Kiddoni moving through the trees. Brock started running, desperate not to let the warrior out of his sight. Yet it was also important not to make a ruckus and draw attention. He watched his steps, trying not to tromp on branches or other things that would crack. This guy was obviously quite capable of using those gnarly-looking weapons behind his shoulder. Brock realized that Kiddoni could easily mistake him for one of those—*what did he call them?*—Gadianton spies. He might turn and attack.

Brock paused to watch Kiddoni run toward an odd-looking bank of twisting trees. The branches created a kind of archway, almost like a tunnel, and it was the route through that part of the woods. He saw Kiddoni pass beneath the arch. Suddenly Brock caught his breath. *Kiddoni was gone!* The Nephite had disappeared right in front of him! For an instant the man was totally transparent and then— *poof!* Nothing!

His mouth still gaping wide, Brock approached the knotted branches of the archway. He walked very slowly, his lungs refusing to breathe and his heart pounding feverishly. He lifted his shoe to take the next step when something extraordinary occurred. The colors blurred and washed before Brock's eyes. The scene *changed!* In just that single step, as he passed beneath that archway of branches, the dull browns and greens of the southern Utah scrub forest transformed into an astonishing rainbow of colors—bright emeralds, flowering reds, and lush yellows.

It was a *jungle!* A rain forest! The transformation jarred his senses so dramatically that Brock lurched backwards and fell onto his rear. As his hind quarter impacted the ground, he blinked, and in that blink, the miracle disappeared. Things became familiar again. He was back in the Utah woods. Glancing up, he saw that he'd thrown himself back across the threshold of twisted branches that comprised the archway. Brock's heartbeat had gone off the charts. His blood burned with adrenaline. Shakily, he got back on his feet. He peered through the archway and into the trees beyond. And then, with all the faith and daring of an eleven-year-old boy, he again crossed beneath the arch.

This time, he'd done it more slowly than before—so slow that he could relish every sensation and vibration as his body crossed over the barrier of a new dimension. The colors again swirled and washed, and the landscape became a tropical paradise: flower-speckled ferns, mossy trees, and leaves as big as umbrellas. The soil under his feet had gone from dusty gray to chocolate black. His nostrils were filled with the musty, vibrant richness of fertile decay and suffocating humidity.

In an instant, Brock's fear became something else. It became *wonder!* His heart still pounded, but this—*this!*—was too incredible for words. And yet he found one. Eyes filled with enchantment, he said "Coooool!" in a long, breathy sigh.

Instantly, Brock turned. He crossed back through the barrier and started running toward his uncle's house. But not in fear. He wasn't fleeing. He just needed a witness, a fellow adventurer, a partner in crime. He had to show this thing—this phenomenon—to Teancum. Or maybe Skyler. Or at the very least, his sister, who may have known about the Nephite, but may not have known about the passageway that entered her new boyfriend's own world.

In his eagerness, Brock sought a shortcut through a thicker section of foliage, having forgotten his earlier lesson when he'd hemmed himself in. The area was rife with shadows and dark corridors. Brock was forced to slow down. A strange feeling settled over him. He paused and checked his back. Had he heard something? He raised up his neck, eyes scanning the deep woods.

Then he saw it—off to the right. There were several dark shapes in the underbrush, seemingly hovering like phantoms. He realized now that the sound he'd heard was *breathing.*

The dark shapes began moving toward him. Brock's blood turned to ice. There were two of them. The warriors wore helmets. The headplates were shaped like skulls; fangs and claws came over the brow and under the chin. The men's faces and bodies were slimed with a thick, red-colored grease. Blood?

The men converged swiftly. Brock tried to back away, ready to turn and flee. But then from behind him a knife blade came around and pressed against his throat.

"Not one sound," growled the low voice of a third blood-covered warrior. *"Not one."*

• • •

Kerra was sure that she was about to emerge from the woods and find the road that would lead out of the hollow and up to her grandfather's shop. She could hear water trickling nearby. When she saw the creek, it was barely wider than her forearm. Then something unusual caught her eye, dangling just above a segment of the creek where the water gathered into a small pool. It struck her as so unusual that she approached for a closer look.

It was an old, weatherworn rope. The rope had been tied around the trunk of the nearby cottonwood, then thrown up over a dead branch. At the other end of the rope, dangling six feet over the pool, was a wind-bleached bone. It looked like a leg bone, though Kerra couldn't have said from what kind of animal. Perhaps a deer or an elk. She might have guessed that a hunter had once hung a carcass here, skinning it with a knife, except . . . the rope was so weird looking, woven with rough threads that she didn't recognize. The workmanship looked homemade. In fact, it looked . . . ancient.

Kerra reached up toward the leg bone, but as her fingers touched the desiccated whiteness, the bone dropped away from the knot in the rope and splashed into the creek. It may have been hanging there for years, but all it needed was Kerra's nudge to finally set it free. She backed away from the splash, but in the process she almost tripped over something at her feet. The thing was nestled in the weeds along the creek bank. Kerra reached down and grabbed it. It felt almost like a metal pipe. As she pulled it out of the mud, she realized with amazement that it was a rifle. A queer, anxious feeling coiled up inside her, like something . . . something forgotten. Kerra knocked some of the mud off the rifle's butt. The stain on the wood had faded, but otherwise it was in fairly good condition.

Then Kerra saw the name etched into the stock: *Chris K. McConnell.*

She stared at those letters for a long time, the creases in her forehead becoming more and more pronounced. *Chris K. McConnell.*

It was her father's name. The rifle had belonged to her *father.* How weird. She swore that she'd seen this firearm once before. That he had shown it to her. Yes, she remembered. He'd shown it to her on the very day that he . . .

Kerra's heart clenched. Her throat seemed to swell, as if she wanted to yell, but all that came out was a painful gasp.

In a single instant, all the realities of Kerra's long and painful life took on a new and alarming interpretation.

• • •

They dragged Brock by the collar into a small, semi-open area in the woods surrounded by sharp briars and the trunks of old, dead trees. Afterwards, they tossed him to the ground. He found himself at the foot of another Gadianton warrior, bringing the total to four. This one was wearing the same strange headplate in the shape of an animal skull, and adorned in the same ragged loincloth and leather chest armor. But unlike the others, who carried long spears with razor-sharp spearheads nearly ten inches in length, this one carried only a bow, as well as a sleek, black knife. Every inch of these men's exposed flesh was caked with the same sticky red substance, like wet, flaking paint. The smell was horrid.

At first Brock's mind was so consumed with terror he couldn't have screamed if he'd tried. However, over the last few minutes, as they'd dragged him deeper into the woods, a

spark of courage had ignited from within. He convinced himself that these men were just bullies—bullies trying to scare
the wits out of him. Brock knew how to deal with bullies.
He'd seen more than his share in California. The worst thing
you could do with bullies was show weakness. They *thrived*
on weakness. He got quickly back to his feet, though his
back was still cornered against the brush.

"Who is he?" asked the newest Gadianton in a gruff
voice.

"Unknown," replied the big, barrel-chested one who'd
held the knife against Brock's throat.

"A Nephite?" asked another. He was the scrawniest of the
four, though to Brock he also seemed to be one of the more
dangerous—as fast as a viper strike.

Sarcastically, the barrel-chested one replied, "Does he
look like a Nephite?"

The last man came forward. He had a cleft upper lip, yet
to Brock it didn't look like a deformity. It appeared as
though he'd inflicted the injury upon himself. "He's one of
the children from that fortress—the one with lights and
music."

"Shut up!" said the one with the gruff voice. Brock was
convinced he was their leader. He looked squarely into the
boy's eyes. "What are you?"

"What *am* I?" Brock replied, stymied.

"Are you a specter? A devil child?"

Brock cocked an eyebrow. "Not the last time I looked."

The villain grabbed the collar of Brock's shirt. "What are
you doing in these woods?"

"Going for a walk. It's a free country." He tried to sound
brave, yet his knees were knocking.

For the first time Brock realized there was a *fifth* man
among them. He was about ten feet away, at the edge of the
brush, kneeling. His face was turned toward the ground and
his hands were bound behind his back. His clothing had the

same ancient flavor—a brown tunic and sandals—but the material was practically in rags, nearly shredded. He was covered with scratches and bruises. This became even more apparent as he raised his eyes for an instant to glance at Brock. A long, scraggly beard, tinged with gray, hung down from his chin. One eye was swollen, and his lip was bleeding—no doubt from abuse that had been inflicted by these men. But who was he? A prisoner? A slave?

Strangely, this man did not seem to Brock to have the same ethnic, Indian sort of appearance as the Gadiantons, or even as the Nephite warrior. In truth, he looked like a standard Caucasian—someone who might be walking on the streets of any American city. That is, any city with homeless vagrants. With his long, unkempt beard, he reminded Brock of guys he'd seen panhandling in Los Angeles.

"Who is *he?*" asked Brock, referring to the captive.

"He is not important," spat the leader. "A slave awaiting death."

"What have you done to him?" Brock persisted.

The Gadianton lost patience. He was here to question, not be questioned. "The same that will be done to you!"

The barrel-chested Gadianton spoke up abruptly. "We're wasting time! Giddianhi will be coming through here in the next—"

"*Silence, Bakaan!*" the leader gruffed. "Are you a complete fool? You will speak in the secret tongue of the Nehors!"

"Sorry, Lord Kush," Bakaan said penitently. He paused for a second, then began talking again. To Brock's astonishment, he continued speaking English, and in precisely the same tone. What was going on? Brock wondered. Did they think he was an idiot?

"Our army will pass through here in a few hours," Bakaan continued. "The escaped slave has been captured.

But the Nephite watchman still lives. We're here to kill any-one who might sound a warning."

"But the Nephite is not at his post," said the smaller, wily-looking Gadianton.

The one with the cleft upper lip barked, "This boy has seen us! Execute him and the slave here and now! Cut their throats."

Brock swallowed hard, terror fully restored inside him. "I won't tell anyone about the army," he said. "I swear I—"

The Gadiantons gaped at him, utterly astonished.

"You understood us?" asked Kush, dumbfounded.

"How could he have understood?" asked Bakaan.

"A demon!" charged the man with the cleft lip.

Kush demanded, "Where did you learn the tongue of the Nehors?"

"I-I couldn't say, really," said Brock sheepishly.

"Slay him!" cried Bakaan. "Cut his throat!"

"You cannot kill a phantom," said the smaller one.

Bakaan pulled a stone knife out of a sheath at his waist. "Watch me."

Brock stiffened in dread as Bakaan's blood-slathered hand reached toward his neck. The boy collapsed to his knees, throwing his arms across his face. But suddenly Kush seized the barrel-chested Bakaan and backed him up against the trunk of one of the dead trees.

"Are you delirious?" Kush raged. "His body would be found here! Warriors of the Nephite army will investigate. The invasion could be revealed!"

The Gadianton with the cleft lip began muttering, "He knows the secret language. He is like the old slave! A sor-cerer of tongues!"

"He's a child of hell!" said Bakaan.

With finality, Kush declared, "Giddianhi will decide."

The argument seemed to be closed, though Bakaan still eyed Brock with clenched malevolence. Kush seized the boy by the hair and yanked him to his feet. The bearded slave was also pulled to his feet and pushed onward, staggering. They were heading southwest. This was all Brock knew. The rest was a mystery. Only the latest of many. Whatever happened, Brock was having difficulty believing that he'd come out of all this with his throat intact.

11

KERRA ENTERED THE VIOLIN SHOP without knocking. She immediately saw her grandfather carving at his bench and approached. Without preliminaries, she set the rifle on the table in front of him.

"It's his, isn't it?" Kerra asked earnestly. But it wasn't a question. More of a declaration. "It belonged to my father. It's his rifle."

Grandpa Lee removed his glasses to take in the whole of it. Then he looked up at Kerra with surprise and dismay. He recognized it, all right. In fact, he'd bought it for his son personally on the boy's sixteenth birthday. He'd been the one who had his name etched onto the stock.

"Where did you find it?" he asked.

Kerra told him about the rope and the wind-bleached bone, then said, "I remember the last time I saw my father he had this rifle in his hands. He was going hunting with some other men. I was five years old, but I remember it like yesterday. Grandpa, who were those other men? Who did he go hunting with that morning?"

Grandpa Lee pondered the question, seemingly trying to collect his thoughts. Then he got up from his bench. "Let's go talk to one of them."

Twenty minutes later, Grandpa Lee and Kerra had driven the old man's rusted Ford pickup across the interstate to the community of Silver Reef. They arrived at the home of Reginald Clacker, a man who'd been a friend of Chris McConnell since high school, a hunting buddy who wasn't known for his boundless ambition. The house was a turn-of-the-nineteenth-century brick and stucco monstrosity that probably should have been condemned well before the end of the twentieth century. Heavyset, balding, and with the usual Budweiser in his fist, he hadn't changed one iota in all these years, Grandpa Lee decided. Chris actually seemed to have outgrown him before he moved to California with Delia. But then came the divorce. The two friends had briefly reunited, along with Fred Beaumont, a lanky descendant of French pioneers to Southern Utah. Shortly thereafter, Chris McConnell had disappeared.

Clacker wouldn't let them into the house. His wife was cooking and didn't appreciate company. They spoke on the porch while several snot-nosed children looked at them from the doorway, along with a snarling yellow Labrador. Clacker examined the rifle that Kerra handed to him.

"Looks like his," Clacker confirmed, scratching his chin. "Where'd you say you found this?"

"In the woods of the hollow," said Kerra. "Grandpa says he was with you the day he disappeared. Is that true?"

"That's right," said Clacker. "Me and Beau picked him up before sunup. We'd seen some deer on the ridge and wanted to see if we could flush a few of 'em out. Thing is, that year we all drew doe tags. Your dad shot a buck. I think ol' Chris just wanted to kill something that day. Didn't matter what."

Clacker's wife called to her husband from inside the

house. "I'm gonna give your supper to the dog if you don't get in here!"

Clacker's face reddened. He snapped back to show who was boss. "Give me a minute, will ya?" He grinned, then continued to Kerra, "I knew his life was a mess. Killing that buck just seemed like the last straw. Like everybody else, I just figured he'd had enough of it all and took off. Started a new life somewhere else." He gave a sideways glance toward the front door. "Sometimes have a notion of doin' that myself."

The conversation ended as the wife announced that the Labrador had stolen a pork chop off his plate.

As Kerra and Grandpa Lee drove home, Kerra's agitation was greater than ever. "Didn't anybody ever search for him?"

"We all searched," said Grandpa sadly. "There was no sign of your father. Nor did we find the deer that he supposedly shot."

Kerra worked up her nerve and said, "Grandpa, you told me yourself that those woods are a special place. An ancient place. Sherilyn and Natasha told me that you claim to have seen ghosts in the hollow, shadows of things from another time. Grandpa, what if my father didn't leave us? What if he didn't run away like my mother always said? What if he accidentally . . . crossed over into some kind of ancient 'realm' and couldn't get back?"

Grandpa Lee gave his granddaughter a strange look. "Crossed over? Ancient 'realm'? What are you—?"

"What if my father has been there for *twelve years?* Stuck in some kind of . . . parallel . . ."

Grandpa Lee could hardly believe this was a real conversation. "Kerra, listen to what you're saying. I know those woods are strange. Yes, I know unusual things happen. And I admit, I've seen some things I can't explain, but—"

Kerra reached under the seat where she'd hidden Kiddoni's carved horn trumpet just before they drove to

Clacker's. She set it on the dashboard in front of her grand-father's nose.

"You haven't seen the half of it, Grandpa," said Kerra. "Things are stranger than you know. A *lot* stranger."

Grandpa Lee gawked at the horn, his mind fully open at last.

• • •

The four Gadiantons continued marching Brock and the bearded prisoner southward, through a narrow canyon. Brock had learned all of their names as they griped and bickered to one another. The leader, Kush, stayed at point while the barrel-chested thug, Bakaan, took every opportunity to shove Brock forward whenever he felt the boy was walking too slowly. The smaller, wiry-looking Gadianton was called Shemish, while the superstitious oaf with the cleft in his upper lip was called Ogath. They had come here to assassinate Kiddoni. Brock felt certain of this. But at the moment the four assassins looked rather confused. They often paused to study the area, as if the surroundings weren't quite familiar. In all honesty, they looked rather lost.

"You guys are from that green, jungle place, right?" Brock asked, still trying to piece all of this into some sort of logical, explainable picture.

The Gadiantons didn't reply. Brock again found himself studying the bearded slave. They'd left his hands bound. A rope was attached to his wrists, which Bakaan held onto like a leash.

"What's your name?" Brock decided to inquire.

The slave replied in a subdued voice, "I am . . . Chris."

The utterance caused Bakaan to strike Chris in the head with the side of his fist. "Don't speak to him," he commanded Brock.

In dismay, Shemish looked around again at their surroundings. "This isn't right."

"Of *course* it's right!" snapped Kush. "It's the same way we came."

So it was true, thought Brock. They *were* lost. It had seemed odd to the boy that they didn't pass beneath another sort of archway or barrier into another dimension, like at the other end of the hollow. He'd predicted that any minute they would reenter the lush, tropical landscape. Could it be that they'd missed the gateway? Was it possible that they were stuck here in the modern century?

At last they emerged from the narrow canyon to see a landscape of alfalfa fields and farm houses. Beyond were the city limits of Leeds, Utah. They'd walked all the way around the hillside and out of his uncle's hollow. The Gadiantons stopped in their tracks as the sight spread out before them.

"By all the gods!" Ogath declared.

Shemish turned angrily to Kush. "I told you it was wrong!"

Brock couldn't hold it in anymore. He started to laugh. "Unbelievable! Wrong turn at Albuquerque, eh?"

"Silence!" growled Kush.

The ever superstitious Ogath pointed a trembling finger at Brock. "It's the demon boy! *He* did this! He *changed* it!"

Bakaan grabbed Brock by front of his shirt and hoisted him to his face. "Where are we? *What have you done?*"

"Nothin'!" Brock insisted. "Don't you get it? Instead of passing back into the dimension with all the jungles, you've stayed right here." He pointed north. "At *that* end of the hollow I can go into your world, and at *this* end, well, it looks like things work just the opposite."

The four warriors gaped at him blankly.

Brock curled up one side of his mouth. "You guys don't watch much *X-Files* or *Outer Limits,* do you?"

Shemish turned to Kush in a panic. "We must find Giddianhi and our army or we will be punished for—"

Kush shoved him back. "Do you think I don't know this?"

Brock noticed that Chris had taken a step forward. He was gazing out at the town, his expression confused, yet pensive, as if he were waking up from a long dream. Or nightmare.

"Leeds," he said absently, almost whispering.

Bakaan yanked his leash and said sharply, "What did you say?"

"Utah," said Chris.

Kush faced him and demanded, "What are these words? What's down there?"

Chris seemed to shake himself back to full alertness. "Nothing. People. Houses."

Surprised, Brock asked him, "Have you been there?"

The bearded slave glanced at Kush, then shook his head. Brock felt sure that he was lying. He was about to call him on it, but then he thought better. Chris must have had a reason.

"Is there food?" Kush demanded.

Chris didn't respond.

Brock decided to step in. "Yeah. There's food. Lots of it." He glanced again at Chris, fearing he may have said the wrong thing, but there was no readable expression on the bearded man's face.

Kush pushed Brock's shoulder with the butt of his spear. "Then take us!"

• • •

Kerra and her grandfather leaned over the carving table in Grandpa Lee's violin shop. Her grandfather had taken out an aerial map of Leeds and the surrounding area—a souvenir he'd obtained from the BLM when his daughter and son-in-law were building their home. The map covered the entire tabletop.

"I know it sounds insane," Kerra repeated. She indicated on the map. "The energy field started right about here, where the crack from the earthquake crosses the hollow. Since then it's spread several hundred yards on either side, all the way up the sides of these two ridges."

"Right along the fault line," said Grandpa thoughtfully.

Kerra continued, "As of last night the area where the two time periods seem to converge includes Uncle Drew's house. But it could grow even wider, Grandpa. For all I know, it could keep growing until it overlaps Leeds and even St. George. Maybe the entire state. Maybe the world!"

Grandpa Lee shook his head again with astonishment. "Unbelievable."

"You don't believe me?" asked Kerra.

"That's just it," said Grandpa Lee. "I *do* believe you. Tell me again—when did this Nephite—?"

"Kiddoni," Kerra clarified.

"Kiddoni. Right. What year did he say it was in his . . . century? Era?"

"He said . . ." Kerra strained to remember. "He said the sixth month of the nineteenth year since the birth of the Messiah."

Grandpa Lee sat down slowly in his work chair, one hand pulling at his beard as his mind strained to get around it all. "Interesting."

"Grandpa, do you think . . . ?" She was almost too afraid to ask, though she knew she had to. The question was practically bursting inside her. "Do you think my father could still be alive?"

Grandpa sighed exhaustedly, painfully. "I don't know." He continued contemplating the year and month that Kerra had mentioned. His eye caught the spine of another old collector's edition of the Book of Mormon on his bookshelf. "I think I'd like to read a little," he said absently.

"What if Kiddoni is right?" asked Kerra, her voice growing ever more urgent. "What if an invasion is really headed this way?"

"Calm down," said Grandpa, his tone not especially calming. "I'm sure no one's in any immediate danger."

• • •

If Brock wasn't freaking out before, he was definitely freaking out now. At present he was walking down a peaceful neighborhood street of Leeds, Utah. At his side were a raggedly dressed bearded man with his hands bound behind his back and four guys with bows and spears whose bodies were slathered in dried blood. No, nothing out of the ordinary for a small Utah town. Surely they saw this type of thing every day! Actually, Brock felt certain that the Gadiantons looked like zombies from an ancient Indian graveyard. Like Aztecs from *Night of the Living Dead*.

The faces of Kush and his cohorts were stunned with awe, thoroughly mesmerized by everything around them. There was also fear in their eyes. Each was tightly gripping his weapons, as if the occupants of these quiet homes might ambush them at any instant.

Brock saw several children floating toy boats in the ditch along the roadside. However, all their playing stopped the moment they caught sight of the town's new visitors. They stood there gaping, letting their boats float away. Shemish locked eyes with a chubby-cheeked eight-year-old boy. The Gadianton's lip curled back to reveal his snarling, rot-blackened teeth. That was too much for the youngster. He made a whimper and turned tail. His friends scampered after him.

Brock turned his head as he heard someone laughing. An old lady in her rocking chair seemed to think the sight of them was the funniest thing she'd ever seen. Even Bakaan's glare couldn't intimidate her. She laughed all the harder. Shemish reached back and started pulling an arrow out of his quiver, determined to silence her for good. Fortunately, Kush stayed his hand.

As they passed by a picket fence, a German shepherd on the other side began barking hysterically. The Gadiantons practically jumped out of their loincloths, adopting full defensive stances. Brock was sure that Ogath would have skewered the mutt with his spear, but just then a GMC Sierra pickup came barreling around the corner. Frantically, the Gadiantons leaped out of the way.

"Get out of the road, morons!" the driver yelled out the window.

The blood-coated assassins watched it drive away, their hearts in their throats.

"A dragon of metal!" Shemish declared in consternation.

Brock noticed that gawking housewives had come to many of the windows.

Ogath stepped up to an old Cadillac Deville parked on the roadside and tapped it with the end of his spear. "This one is dead," he declared.

Once again, Kush seized Brock by the scruff of the neck. He'd seen enough. His tour of the twenty-first century was over. "You will find us food and take us back to where we were! Understand?"

Brock nodded. He caught Chris's eye over Kush's shoulder. He could tell that the bearded man's mind was turning, alert for any opportunity he could create to escape. But with his hands bound behind his back, what could he do? Brock felt he couldn't depend on Chris. *This is up to me,* he thought, and frankly, right now he was having a serious shortage of ideas. Whatever they did, it would have to be soon. Otherwise, one of these Utah rednecks might just grab a shotgun and take matters into his own hands. That might not have been so bad, except that Bakaan was keeping him so near that Brock was sure he'd be caught in any crossfire.

In the distance the boy could see the town's only restaurant and convenience store. After a sigh of trepidation, he began leading them toward it.

12

KERRA WALKED HASTILY BACK toward the farm-house down the long driveway, her thoughts still caught up in a hailstorm of anxiety. Grandpa Lee's counsel was to hold off warning her aunt and uncle until he could do a little research in the Book of Mormon. She still carried Kiddoni's ancient horn in her hand. Kerra thought of her Nephite, wondering if he'd reached his destination. She peered into the foliage of the hollow, eyes searching for movement—shadows of the men that Kiddoni and her cousin Tessa had described. It was the silence in the woods that made her the most uneasy. She quickened her pace.

As Kerra approached the house, she saw Teancum on the front porch, looking terribly bored.

"Where's Brock?" she asked.

Teancum cocked an eyebrow. "Isn't he with you?"

Just then Aunt Corinne came out of the front door. On her face was a look of determination, as if she'd made a decision.

"Kerra," she said soberly. "We need to talk."

Kerra ignored her, still focused on Teancum. "What do you mean 'with me'?"

"He saw you leave this morning. I watched him get out of bed and slip on his shoes. I think he was going to follow you."

A cold chill climbed Kerra's spine. Alarm bells were ringing in her brain. She turned and began running back up the driveway.

"Kerra!" Corinne called in frustration. "KERRA!"

But Kerra continued around the bend. Soon she reached her pathway into the woods. Within seconds, she melted into the undergrowth. Neither Corinne nor Teancum had pursued her far enough to watch her leave the road. Nevertheless, Kerra had been seen.

Only seconds after she'd entered the woods, the chrome wheels of a black Acura NSX-T stopped on the very spot where she'd left the driveway. Hitch Ventura gazed toward the place where Kerra had disappeared. His three favorite henchmen, Adder, Prince, and Dushane, were also inside the vehicle.

"Well, well," he said, thrilled at the prospect of finding Kerra isolated and alone so soon. He crushed out his cigarette and started to open his car door.

"Need any company?" asked Adder from the backseat.

"Nah," said Hitch. A twisted grin climbed his face. "This might, uh, require some privacy."

Dushane snickered. The others smiled.

"Secure the house," Hitch commanded. "Find that gym bag."

• • •

Corinne wasn't quite sure what she ought to do. That social worker, Mr. Paulson, had tried to call again, but

Corinne saw the Caller I.D. and didn't answer. Apparently he wasn't going to give up. He might even send the police. It would be better, she decided, if she laid it all out with Kerra. Her first fear was that Kerra might feel betrayed, that she might run away and never return. Corinne couldn't bear that. Yet the fact was, there was a stolen car in her garage. She had to convince Kerra to go to the police on her own. Corinne would stay by her side. She would fight for her and, God willing, she might even make it possible for Kerra and Brock to stay with them permanently. Oh, if only the good Lord would allow a miracle like that! However, to her frustration, she couldn't seem to pin Kerra down long enough to have a conversation. As she placed the plates from lunch into the dishwasher, she decided that she would pull the girl aside right after dinner. But just as she made this decision, the front door flew open.

In rushed Teancum in a panic, as if he were trying to get away from someone. But before he could close the front door again, someone's boot kicked it open. In stormed three men in their late teens and early twenties, all of them wearing bandannas, dressed in leather and denim, and with enough earrings between them to build a dog chain. But the thing that caught the children's attention—the thing which stopped Corinne's heart—was what they were carrying in their hands: handguns and automatic weapons.

The girls playing in the front room shrieked.

"All right!" shouted the one with sunglasses and a black goatee. "Everybody! Gather 'round! We're gonna play a game! It's called sit down, shut up, and nobody gets their head blown off. *Everyone!* NOW!"

Corinne reached for the phone, but before she could hit 911, someone's hand grabbed the phone cord and ripped it out of the wall. Corinne turned to see the gangster's face. It was cut by a terrible scar; one of his eyes couldn't seem to focus right. He took the receiver from Corinne's hand, then grinned and shook his finger at her, as if scolding a small child.

Corinne caught a glimpse of her son Skyler through the kitchen window. He was peeking around the side of the garage, having heard all the commotion. However, upon seeing that the house was under siege, he shrank back inside, hiding. Corinne realized she and her children were alone and helpless.

She said to the one with sunglasses, trying hard to put a bite in her voice, "My husband will be home any minute."

"Cool," said the gangster. "The more the merrier."

"What do you want with us?" demanded Corinne.

At last he removed his sunglasses. "I'm so glad that you asked."

•   •   •

The bell jingled as Brock walked through the front door of Molly's Restaurant and Market. He was followed by Chris, still dressed in ancient rags, still with his hands bound. After him entered the four Gadiantons, spears and swords still raised and ready in case anyone gave them trouble. If he hadn't feared for his life, Brock might have died of embarrassment. The scene must have looked utterly ridiculous.

The mini-market part of the establishment lay right of the doorway, while the restaurant, with about four booths and an equal number of tables, was off to the left. A few more than a dozen customers were present, divided equally between shoppers and diners. Every single person stopped in midbite or midsentence to gawk. A teenage waitress and a customer the same age started giggling.

Another teenage girl behind the cash register was also finding it hard to suppress her laughter as she asked, "Can I help you?"

The Gadiantons stood thunderstruck at the sheer quantity

of potato chip bags, donut trays, hot dogs, and candy. Their mouths watered at the smell of hamburgers and hot grease from the kitchen. As skinny as several of these Gadiantons were, Brock realized they might actually be starving. Ogath, in particular, almost looked delirious with excitement, not quite sure where to begin.

An older man in a white shirt and crumpled tie, who Brock guessed was the store's owner or manager, approached from an office in back. He looked his new customers up and down. "You all with the Manti Pageant?"

Shemish and Ogath were already sniffing the bread loaves and fruit pies through the plastic packaging. Bakaan walked up to one of the booths in the restaurant where a heavyset kid of thirteen or so was chowing down on a cheeseburger, though he hadn't taken a bite since the Gadiantons had entered the store. The burger was scrunched in his fingers, his mouth hanging open. Bakaan brought up his saw-bladed sword threateningly, then grabbed the cheeseburger right out of the boy's hands. Holding it sideways, he tried to shove the entire sandwich into his mouth, coating his nose and chin with mustard and grease.

Chris, who stood nearest the manager, tried to whisper to him discreetly. "Call the police."

Kush barked to his fellow Gadiantons, "Take the food! All you can carry!"

As Bakaan wolfed down the rest of the cheeseburger, he held his weapon aggressively, narrowly watching the other customers, daring anyone to make the slightest move. Ogath tore apart a potato chip bag, sending its contents flying. Shemish snatched up a grimy-looking waste can with several wads of chewing gum stuck around the edge. He pulled out the liner, half full of garbage, and flung it down the aisle. Then he began piling groceries inside, including dumping in each plate of hot grub belonging to the diners.

Finally, a husky trucker in a Diamondbacks baseball cap

had had enough. He grabbed for Bakaan. But the wily assassin saw it coming. He snapped back the butt of his spear, whacking the man directly in the face. The trucker went down hard, fully unconscious, with a bull's eye-shaped bruise swelling on his forehead. The waitress and several other customers started to scream. A few people in the market area made a break for the door. The manager reached for the phone beside the cash register, frenetically punching numbers.

"We go!" yelled Kush.

He pushed Chris toward the door. Brock noticed a rear entrance and started toward it, but Ogath caught him by the hair and yanked him back. The boy screeched in fury and pain as the cleft-lipped Gadianton dragged him toward the front door.

As they emerged, Brock could see customers in the parking lot scrambling to climb into their vehicles. Several cars were screeching away. The faces of Bakaan and Shemish were stuffed to overflowing with food.

Kush grabbed Brock's arm and stood him upright. He indicated the various parked cars. "You know these machines?"

Brock nodded.

"You will take us in one of these," Kush commanded.

Ogath reacted swiftly to achieve his leader's objective and approached a four-door Crown Victoria into which a man and his wife were rapidly climbing. The wife was already closing the door, but the man was just hoisting in his leg as Ogath seized him by the shoulders and tossed him out onto the pavement. The woman, screaming frantically, abandoned the car of her own accord. Kush pushed Brock toward the door.

"Wait!" said Chris. He turned sideways, revealing his bound hands and said to Kush, "Cut me loose. He's a kid. He can't drive."

Brock opened his mouth to protest, but then he caught Chris's stern and pleading glance. He got the message.

"He's right," said Brock. "I can't drive."

Kush narrowed his eyes with suspicion. They could hear a police siren somewhere in the distance. Kush growled resentfully. What Chris had said must have seemed true. No other cars were being driven by children. These machines were obviously meant for adults.

Chris saw Ogath leaning over the man he'd thrown onto the pavement. The assassin had drawn a knife! He was going to cut the man's throat!

"NO!" Chris shouted. "Or I won't drive it! I swear I won't help you!"

Ogath looked at Kush, who nodded for him to back away. Disappointed, Ogath shoved the man back onto the pavement. The man tried to crawl away, trembling feverishly and blubbering like a child. Kush cut Chris's bonds using his black-bladed knife. As Chris massaged his wrists, the Gadianton leader pressed the knife to his neck.

"Try something and I will not hesitate," Kush seethed.

As Shemish realized there was no room for the trash can, he simply dumped it out onto the backseat. He, Ogath, and Bakaan climbed in back, pushing the food into the foot space, eating as they went. Brock was forced to sit between them. Chris and Kush sat up front, Kush still threatening with his knife. The woman ran to her husband and helped him to his feet. As the Crown Victoria spun around and drove onto the street, several Gadianton spears were hanging out the windows.

Chris headed away from town, away from the approaching police siren, away from all the commotion. Brock watched Chris with greater curiosity than ever before. The bearded slave certainly seemed comfortable behind the wheel of a car. He'd saved the life of that man on the pavement. Who was this person? Brock felt sure now that he was not from the time period of the Gadiantons. But where had he come from?

It wasn't long before Brock was covered in Doritos and donut crumbs as the Gadiantons on either side persisted in devouring as much as their stomachs could hold.

"What is this?" asked Shemish as he tore open one of the plastic bags and pulled out a long gummy worm.

"Candy," said Brock.

As Shemish bit the worm in half, his face puckered up and he spat it against the window.

"That's the really sour kind," Brock told him.

Chris turned onto the dirt road that eventually led to Grandpa Lee's violin shop and down into the hollow. Brock found this action the most curious of all. Chris seemed to know exactly where was going. If only he could have asked him questions, but this was neither the time nor place.

"Where are you taking us?" Kush barked at the driver.

"Back where we came from," Chris replied.

"Don't trust him," said Bakaan. "He has defied us! He has offended Lord Giddianhi. He must die!"

Brock noticed Ogath do a double take. The assassin was gazing out the side window of the car. Brock stared across the sagebrush in the same direction, trying to see what had drawn his attention. Then he blinked in consternation. For a fraction of an instant, the scenery seemed to transform. It was just a flash—a wash of colors. But in that flash, Brock perceived the same lush jungle that he had seen when he'd passed beneath the archway in the forest. Seconds later, a jagged wall of energy, like a prism of pale, transparent light, seemed to shoot up from the ground just left of the road, steadily growing brighter. It was like peering through the heat vapors on a long highway, or through the waters of a massive aquarium. On the other side of those vapors were hazy images of a tropical forest. Everyone had seen the phenomenon now, including Chris. He glanced over at Kush in the neighboring seat to confirm that he was fully distracted. Then Chris turned the wheel sharply. Brock was thrown to one side, his body squished by the weight of the three Gadiantons around him. The Crown Victoria careened off the dirt road, bouncing over a narrow ditch, smashing a barb-wire fence post, and crashing into the sagebrush. The car was headed straight for the jagged wall of energy!

Kush, his eyes full of fury, turned back to Chris, raising the long blade of his knife to strike. Brock was certain that Chris was a dead man. Kush was already in mid-swing. But at that instant the car passed through the wall. What happened next surprised Brock McConnell more than anything he'd seen thus far.

Kush disappeared. In fact, all *four* Gadiantons vanished as quickly as if someone had blown out a match. Kush's long knife blade seemed to pass right through Chris's neck, but in the next blink of an eye, Brock and Chris were alone. The ancient spears and weapons were also gone. The Crown Victoria crashed over the lip of a ravine. The headlights impacted a mound of dirt. Brock and Chris were jolted forward as the car stopped cold. The boy pushed open the door and climbed outside, his feet unsteady. Chris did the same, coughing in the cloud of dust. Both could hear a strange humming in the air, like thousands of crickets, incessant and screeching.

Brock stumbled back up the ravine—back toward the wall of energy they'd just passed through. He realized the energy was emitted from a crack, a crooked fissure in the earth. The two- to-four-inch wide fissure bent around and went northward, disappearing in the sagebrush. Presumably it meandered into the trees about fifty yards farther. This, Brock knew, was the southernmost end of the hollow. As Brock moved closer to the swirling, watery wall, he began to hear surreal echoes—the voices of Kush, Bakaan, and the others. Then, in a flash, he saw them.

The four Gadianton assassins were visible just across the fissure, in the midst of a backdrop of jungle and moss-covered forest. The image shimmered in and out of focus, blending with the backdrop of the Utah desert. For a moment the images of the two time periods appeared to be matted on top of each other, like a dissolve in a movie. The Gadiantons were on the ground, awkwardly trying to regain their footing. They looked cut and bruised, covered with dirt and leaves. Brock was speechless with amazement. As Chris had driven through that wall of energy, the Gadiantons had somehow "fallen" back into their own world. *Incredible!* The inertia of the automobile had actually sent them tumbling and rolling in the tropical undergrowth. Brock glanced back at Chris. Why hadn't *he* fallen back? Brock knew the answer without much pondering. It was because the bearded man in tattered clothing belonged *here*. Chris belonged in the twenty-first century, whereas the Gadiantons . . .

Brock realized Kush had seen him. The shark-eyed assassin was peering back at him through the wall of energy. Bakaan had seen him too. Bakaan snatched up his spear and lunged at Brock, eyes full of hatred. Brock might have scrambled backwards, but it was too late. He braced himself for death.

But the spear point did not penetrate his flesh. What crossed over the fissure was only a gossamer wisp—a mere "shadow" of the spear. For some reason, Bakaan's weapon could not cross the barrier of energy. Brock lowered his arms and gaped at Bakaan and Kush. He and the others started ranting furiously and yelling, their voices subdued and hollow-sounding, as if they were far, far away.

Brock was startled by Chris's hand, grasping his shoulder.

"Let's go." His tone was full of urgency.

But Brock couldn't tear his eyes away from the watery image.

"What happened to them?" he asked.

"This isn't their world," Chris explained. "They can't pass through here."

Brock shook his head in consternation. "I don't get it."

"Some places are entrances. Some are exits. And some—like this—are just windows. But you can't predict it—how it will change, how powerful it will grow, or when it will disappear. C'mon! We have to cross the hollow!"

Brock looked at Chris in wonder. How did he know such things? Where did he gain his experience with this phenomenon? But Chris was already striding back down the slope of the ravine. He waved again for Brock to follow. Brock started down the hill, but then he glanced back one last time. When he did, he saw something that made his heart stop. In the jungle beyond Kush, Bakaan, Shemish, and Ogath, he could see *more* Gadiantons—*hundreds* of them! All were covered in blood and armed to the teeth with swords, spears, and bows. They were marching straight at them!

But then, as if someone had suddenly yanked the cord on a window blind, the "window" of energy was sucked back into the fissure. Once again all Brock could see were the sagebrush and red rock hills of southern Utah. But Brock's mind didn't believe it. The Gadiantons were still there. He may not have been able to see them now, but they were still coming. And they were marching toward the hollow.

Chris paused to let Brock catch up, and the two of them ran headlong into the woods.

"It's true," Brock said to Chris. "You *are* from here. I mean, from *today*—from *my time*."

Chris, still running, glanced over at Brock. "What's your name, boy?"

"Brock McConnell."

Suddenly the bearded man stopped. Brock stopped as well.

Chris was gaping at him, his face almost white with shock. He panted and seemed to be gathering his wits. "What did you say?"

"Brock McConnell." Brock wasn't quite sure what to make of the man's expression. Awkwardly, he added, "My uncle's house is about a mile from here, through these woods."

Chris reached up his hand, trembling slightly, and touched the boy's face. "How old are you?"

"Eleven," Brock replied.

The bearded man's voice cracked with emotion as he asked, "You have a sister?"

A strange feeling spread over Brock. He nodded. "Kerra."

"Sakerra?"

"Yeah," said Brock, his head now cocked, eyes squinting, as he tried to figure out what was going on. Why was the bearded man acting this way? "How did you know that?"

He realized that Chris's eyes were full of tears. But before Chris could answer the boy's question, the drone of the Whistlers began to escalate in volume. Chris straightened up, suddenly very alert and looking around in alarm.

"They're coming," he declared. "We have to keep moving!"

He took the boy's hand and led him again through the trees.

• • •

Grandpa Lee sat at his desk, pouring all of his concentration into the verse of scripture in front of him. He mumbled the words of Third Nephi, chapter 4, verse 7 with growing astonishment.

" . . . *and it was in the sixth month; and behold, great and terrible was the day that they did come up to battle; and they were girded about after the manner of robbers; and they had a lamb-skin about their loins, and they were dyed in blood, and their heads were shorn, and had headplates upon them; and great and terrible was the appearance of the armies of Giddianhi . . ."*

He looked up from the book. "Sixth month. Nineteenth year."

Grandpa Lee shuddered. If it was true, and if Kerra was right, something terrible was about to happen. Something menacing and evil. He also realized it was something that might march right through his daughter's front yard.

● ● ●

Brock cried out in terror. There were ghosts in the woods! The shadows of blood-covered wraiths appeared and disappeared to the right and left and sometimes right in front of them, causing both him and Chris to veer another direction.

Chris continued to grasp Brock's arm as they made their way over a small bluff. Below them now was a stagnant pond with dozens of dead trees growing out of the mud. The branches, whitened by alkali, had a strange, skeletal appearance that accented the mood of death and horror created by the Gadianton ghosts. They moved swiftly around its banks. Chris appeared to be headed directly toward the home of Brock's aunt and uncle.

Suddenly Chris jolted to a stop. In a shadowy pocket of foliage directly in front of them something coalesced from the darkened brush. A Gadianton warrior!—one they'd never seen before! He was charging directly at them, weapon drawn.

Instinctively, Chris tried to move in front of the boy, but Brock was already diving out of the way. The Gadianton barreled into Chris's chest and drove him off the bluff. For an instant the two of them were caught in the air, at last landing with an explosive splash in the oily black waters of the pond. Brock looked on, his stomach in his mouth, as Chris fought the Gadianton with his fists, using the Gadianton's own shield to fend off a lethal blow from his attacker's obsidian-edged sword.

Chris saw Brock on the bluff above him. "Run!" he screamed.

But Brock hesitated. The Gadianton would surely kill him! It seemed certain! Just then another blood-painted warrior materialized from the woods to his right. Brock slipped behind some leafy brambles to avoid being seen. The second Gadianton leaped off the bluff and into the water to aid his comrade. Brock had almost decided to join in the fight, knowing full well that he'd probably be killed. But there was something about that bearded man who knew his sister's name. The feeling made Brock actually wonder if trying to save this man's life was a cause worth dying for. But then another Gadianton coalesced from the woods. And another. The forest was *alive* with Gadianton warriors. Joining in the fight was no longer an act of courage, but one of suicide. Brock wouldn't even reach the water's edge before he was struck down. His heart was breaking in half, yet he backed away through the brush, crawling on his hands and knees. At last he got to his feet and started running again toward the farmhouse. He had to get help. If there was any hope of saving Chris, he needed to return with men and guns. Oh, how he'd enjoy watching the reaction in a Gadianton's eyes as he stared down a shotgun barrel!

He ran faster than he'd ever run before, dodging branches and brush at every step, all the while seeing Chris's face in his mind and hearing Chris's voice as he asked Brock to repeat his name. The boy still wouldn't draw any conclusions. The very notion frightened him. He knew only that saving Chris's life might turn out to be the most important act of his life.

13

KERRA HAD ARRIVED AT THE CLEARING, the ancient horn still in her hands. She crossed over the fissure and looked around anxiously.

"Brock!" she shouted, then waited impatiently for a response from the woods.

She heard a sound in the brush behind her. Kerra turned, anticipating her brother's face. But instead she met the eyes of Hitch Ventura. She could feel her blood go cold.

Hitch grinned. "What a surprise! Could it really be Kerra McConnell? You don't look all too thrilled to see me."

Kerra backed away. "What are you doing here, Hitch? How did you find us?"

"Your little bro invited us." He moved closer, hemming her in against the bushes on the western edge of the clearing. "He has something for me."

"He has *nothing* for you," she spat. "Leave here!"

But Hitch only leaned in closer, as if sniffing her perfume. Then he raised his hands descriptively and said, "Brown leather bag. 'Bout yea big. Seen it?"

Kerra *did* remember such a bag. She remembered seeing it in Teancum's bedroom the first day they arrived, packed inside Brock's larger duffel bag. It had crossed her mind to ask Brock what it was, but then she'd forgotten about it. Hitch noted her reaction.

"Ah, so you *have* seen it."

She reached into the brush, found a dead branch, and easily broke it off. Then she brought it between them threateningly. Hitch backed off half a step, but he only seemed amused. He shook his head, making a "tsk, tsk" sound with his tongue.

"Always so unfriendly." He blew a sad sigh, as if deeply hurt.

"What's in this bag?" Kerra demanded.

"Nothin' much," said Hitch, shrugging. Then he narrowed his gaze. "Only a quarter million dollars—street value." He moved closer again.

Kerra raised back the stick. "I'm warning you . . ."

He made a heavy, mocking frown. "Ah, come on now. I promise you have nothing to worry—"

Hitch broke off his own sentence and made a surprise lunge to seize her. But Kerra had read the change in his eyes. She smashed the stick into his face. Hitch cried out and staggered back, a long, red gash now visible on his cheek, bleeding. He touched the wound with his fingers. When he saw the blood, his temper erupted.

Kerra tried to run from the clearing, but she made it only five steps before Hitch landed on her spine and smashed her to the ground. As he tackled her, the horn bounced into the weeds. Hitch grabbed her hair and shirt and viciously flipped her onto her back like a sack of grain. Kerra desperately tried again to swing the stick, but Hitch was too powerful—too angry. He stripped it from her hands. She struggled in vain as one of his knees pinned her left arm. The other knee pinned her right arm. She looked up into his gleaming, flaming eyes, the blood from his injury now streaming down his chin and neck.

"You like to struggle?" he asked. "That's just fine."

Kerra let out a wail of hatred and fury. She wanted to gouge his eyes out, scratch the flesh from his already bleeding face. But he'd rendered her utterly helpless. There was nothing she could do. One of his palms pressed down hard on her mouth and nose. Kerra's mind clouded over with terror. But then her eyes flew wide. A shape appeared over Hitch's shoulder. A person!

It was Kiddoni!

Kerra watched as his powerful hands latched onto the shirt on either side of Hitch's neck. He pulled him off her and tossed him hard into a thicket of mesquite.

Dazed and disoriented, Hitch looked up from the midst of the briars and focused his eyes on—*what?* It was a man dressed in—what was it? Animal hide and leather? A stone weapon behind his shoulder? Hitch shook himself. This couldn't be right.

Kiddoni was still glowering down on him, awaiting his next move. Hitch sprang to his feet.

He cursed as he asked, "Who are you?"

"The thing you fear in the dark," Kiddoni replied.

Hitch drew something from his pocket. He pressed a button, and a cold steel blade shot out and snapped in place. "I doubt that very much."

Hitch sprang from the nest of mesquite, stabbing at Kiddoni. Kiddoni dodged the knife, then reached back and drew the sword from behind his shoulder. Using the flat side of the blade, he knocked Hitch in the back of the head. The gangster sank to the ground, visibly unconscious.

Kiddoni helped Kerra to her feet. She arose, her expression full of awe, and threw her arms around his neck. "Oh, Kiddoni!"

The Nephite looked at the fallen gangster. "Who is he?"

"No one," said Kerra. "A flea. A gnat. I'm so glad to see you."

She kissed him, and wouldn't have stopped, but Kiddoni stood her back and said seriously, "I couldn't convince them, Sakerra. I told them about the Gadianton spy, but I couldn't report that I had seen him with my own eyes. They wouldn't listen. Their heads are like granite. They're still convinced Giddianhi will invade from the mountains near the river, and in the springtime—just as the Lamanites have done countless times in the past." He reached down and took up the shield that he'd leaned against the rock.

Kerra suddenly remembered why she was here. "Kiddoni, Brock is missing!"

"Your brother? How long?"

From the corner of her eye, Kerra saw a twitch in Hitch's body. What happened next was so quick that she hardly had time to react.

"Watch out!" she screamed.

Hitch had reached into his jacket and found a handgun. Since he'd obviously preferred a switchblade, it hadn't occurred to Kerra that he might have a firearm. Kiddoni turned and stared curiously down the barrel of the gun—unsure what it was. Hitch pulled the trigger. The barrel flashed. A splintered hole appeared in Kiddoni's shield. The bullet went right through. The impact blasted Kiddoni backwards. He landed in the brush, unmoving.

"KIDDONI!" Kerra became hysterical. She tried to go to him, but Hitch was back on his feet. He grabbed her arm.

Tears shot from Kerra's eyes. *"No! Kiddoni! NO!"*

The gangster's hold was firm. He dragged her roughly through the trees, leaving the Nephite's body on the forest floor.

At the instant of the gunshot, Brock had been running through the woods, keeping himself ahead of the Gadianton army. He sensed instinctively that the shot had come from the clearing where he'd first seen Kiddoni. Fearing for his sister, Brock altered course.

Grandpa Lee also heard the shot. At the moment, he was making his way down the driveway. Upon hearing the blast, he briskly continued toward the farmhouse. But then he stopped again as he heard Kerra's voice and rustling in the brush. Quickly, he moved off the road.

Hitch emerged from the trees, still dragging Kerra and holding her wrists to keep from getting punched in the face. The wound on Hitch's face was still bleeding. Added to the blood was some bright purple swelling, making him now look more like a ghoul than a gangster.

Grandpa Lee watched him haul Kerra onto the front porch. Prince opened the front door and met them.

"What happened?" Prince asked, finding it hard to suppress a smile. Obviously Hitch had had some girl trouble.

"I'm fine!" Hitch snapped back. "I killed someone. An Indian. *Something!* Did you get the bag?"

Adder, just inside the door with his AK-47 rifle, replied, "We haven't found it yet. Or the kid."

Grandpa Lee saw several other gangsters through the front window. He quickly turned and entered the woods.

Inside the house, Hitch shoved Kerra into the only empty chair in the living room. The Whitman family, minus Uncle Drew, were seated around the living room, holding and comforting one another. The smaller children looked terrified, while Corinne maintained an expression of reticent defiance. Also missing was Skyler. Corinne glanced out the window toward the garage now and then, praying fervently that her son wouldn't do anything foolish.

Hitch leaned down to stare into Kerra's face. His patience was gone. His rage was ready to explode in a way that it had never done before. "Where is your brother? Where is that bag?"

Kerra was still overwhelmed with grief, still at the edge

of hysteria. She pleaded with Hitch, "Please! Let me go back! Let me help him!"

"He's *dead!*" Hitch barked. "It's *over!* Tell me what I want to know or I'll make it happen to someone else!"

Corinne realized that Dushane had seen something out the window. He was looking toward the garage.

Dushane turned toward Adder. "Someone's out there!"

Adder rushed to the side door. Corinne jumped up, but Prince restrained her.

"No!" she cried.

Skyler was in the act of creeping across the driveway, trying to make it into the trees, as the side door flew open. Adder discharged a short blast from his automatic weapon. The bullets hit the gravel in front of the teenager, scattering the stones. Skyler stopped cold in his tracks and threw up his arms, his knees shaking like Jell-O.

With mock politeness, Adder asked, "Would you like to come inside and join the party?"

• • •

Brock was panting like a puffer fish. He couldn't have said how far ahead of the Gadiantons he'd managed to get, but it had been ten minutes since he'd seen the last warrior or ghost. Shortly, he emerged from the trees and saw the stone and log in the clearing's center. Beyond the stone, lying in the brush, was the very sight he'd been dreading. A body. But it wasn't his sister. It was the body of the Nephite. He approached cautiously, uncertain if this man was really any less dangerous than Bakaan or the others. Brock stopped abruptly. Kiddoni started to stir.

The Nephite opened his eyes. The first thing he focused on was the boy, standing about five feet away.

"Brock?" he asked weakly.

The boy nodded. "You're the man who was with my sister, right?"

Before Kiddoni could answer, someone else entered the clearing. Both of them turned their heads in alarm, but it was only Grandpa Lee. He went immediately to Kiddoni. The Nephite's strength seemed to be gathering. He tried to sit up.

"Unbelievable," Grandpa said. He knelt down to help the Nephite. "Where are you hit?"

Brock stepped forward to offer a hand. They helped Kiddoni take off his chest armor. The boy remained terribly anxious about Chris. He tried to point toward the woods to the south. "Grandpa Lee, we have to get help. There's a man back there—"

But the old man's attention was riveted on the Nephite. "One emergency at a time," he told his grandson.

"What hit me?" asked Kiddoni.

"A bullet, I'm afraid," said Grandpa Lee. "But I can't see exactly where . . . Well, lookee here." He raised up the chest armor. "You, my friend, have the luck of the Irish."

The bullet was imbedded in the back of the armor. It had only grazed Kiddoni's side. His wound looked black and nasty, but it was hardly bleeding, as if the wound were almost self-cauterizing. Lee dug out the warped piece of metal and showed it to Kiddoni.

"There's your slug. You've never seen one of those, I'd wager."

Kiddoni struggled to stand. "Where's Kerra?"

The tone of his question made it plain to Brock that something had happened to her. "Is something wrong?" he asked.

"He took her," said Kiddoni. "The man with the weapon that threw the bullet." The Nephite gathered up his spear and bow and started walking determinedly toward the farmhouse.

Grandpa Lee grabbed his shoulder. "Wait. These people have more guns. More bullets—"

"I will rescue her," said Kiddoni, undeterred.

Grandpa sighed, realizing his determination. "Then let us help you."

· · ·

"*A quarter million dollars!*" Hitch screamed into Kerra's face.

She was still seated in the chair. Aunt Corinne and the children, including Skyler, were also present, under the watchful and fidgeting eye of Adder. Hitch's yelling had brought little Bernadette and five-year-old Sariah to tears. Corinne tried to comfort them, but her efforts weren't working very well. Hitch continued pacing, holding an ice-filled rag to his cheek and rubbing the bump on the back of his head.

"The purest grade Colombian on the West Coast!" he kept ranting. "That weasel, Spree, stole it from us!"

Prince and Dushane also looked nervous and edgy.

"How long are we gonna wait?" asked Prince.

"As long as it takes!" Hitch snapped back.

"What if the kid saw us comin' and ditched?" asked Adder.

Hitch looked at Kerra again. He narrowed his eyes as he said, "Then I'll start shooting someone every—"

The threat was interrupted by a honk from a car horn. Everybody looked up in surprise—especially the gangsters. The honk had come from *their own Acura!*

Hitch turned to Prince and Dushane. "Check it out!"

The pair went hurriedly toward the front door, weapons ready to blaze. They threw open the door and moved forward until they could clearly see the black sports car, parked just down the drive. The passenger door was open wide.

They glanced at one another, wondering which idiot of the three of them had been responsible for leaving it unlocked. Somebody appeared to be sitting in the driver's seat, but the dark tint on the windshield prevented them from discerning any features. The gangsters drew closer, fingers tight on the triggers. But as they finally saw into the passenger door, they were greeted by the wide smile of Grandpa Lee.

"Hello!" he said ebulliently. Lee saw the guns pointed into the car and asked, "You sure you wanna use those? Might mess up this fine upholstery."

Prince and Dushane clenched their teeth furiously. They simultaneously moved into position to reach inside and drag the old man out onto the pavement.

Suddenly, Kiddoni arose from the opposite side of the car, gripping his long, thick spear in the middle. As the pair of henchmen straightened their backs to see him, the Nephite did a double hit—smacking Dushane in the head with the blunt end while smashing Prince with the side of the stone tip. Dushane went down like an oak. Prince staggered. He pulled the trigger on the AK-47, but his aim was reckless. The burst of bullets blew out the Acura's back window. Finally, he dropped the gun and folded over, holding his head. But he still hadn't collapsed. As he staggered close to the passenger door, Grandpa Lee gave the door a stiff push and finished the job. Prince crumpled to the ground.

Hitch stood inside the front door of the farmhouse. The Acura was just outside his range of vision. He wasn't about to come out any farther—not after hearing the gunfire. He had no desire to catch a stray bullet between the eyes.

"Prince?" he called out. "Dushane?"

There was no response. Hitch glanced back at Adder, also terribly tense. The family looked more terrified than ever. At last Hitch leaned outside far enough to see his car. Dushane was sprawled out beside it, unconscious. His tongue was actually hanging out of his mouth, just like in a cartoon. Another pair of legs was also visible—those belonging to Prince. Not another soul was in sight. Prince's and Dushane's weapons weren't visible either. Whoever had attacked them had also taken their gats. Hitch was beside himself. *What had just happened?*

He quickly slipped back inside, panic evident in his eyes. He faced Kerra and rest of the family. "Tell me what's going on?!"

They just stared at him. Adder looked as jittery as ever. Hitch grabbed Kerra and yanked her to her feet. He put his 38-Special to her throat, then stood her between himself and the window, using her as a shield.

"Who's out there?" Hitch demanded, his voice cracking with desperation.

Kerra shook her head. She was no less astonished by what was happening than everyone else. Had a wounded Kiddoni convinced some fellow Nephites to come into these woods to check things out? Was it Gadianton warriors? Were they on the prowl for whatever victims they could lay their hands on?

Hitch peered out the window again, careful to keep Kerra in front of him. Kerra suddenly gasped. She'd caught a glimpse of her brother's shirt. Brock was hiding behind the shell of the old rusted Cadillac in the weeds beyond the driveway. Hitch had seen him too. He pulled Kerra toward the side door and shouted back at Adder, "Keep everyone in this room! Don't let anybody move!"

Still using her as a human shield, Hitch moved outside, quickly checking the area in all directions. He hurried across the driveway toward the Cadillac, clutching Kerra's arm. She wanted to shout a warning—shout anything!—but if Brock tried to run now, he'd be an easy target. As they arrived at the rusted Cadillac, Hitched reached through the weeds and underneath the shell. He seized Brock's shirt and dragged him out of his hiding place. Brock's hands were clenched, ready to lash out at his assailant, but then he saw his sister and the gun.

"Where is it?" Hitch demanded, wasting no more time.

"Huh?" asked Brock.

Hitch struck the boy in the ear with the pistol butt.

"Hitch, don't!" cried Kerra.

"Spree's bag!" Hitch clarified. He put the pistol to the boy's temple. "Where is it? Don't lie to me."

"I-I hid it!" Brock squeaked. "In the woods!"

At that instant Hitch spotted Kiddoni, sword in hand and bow over his shoulder. The Nephite ran from behind the house to the rear of the garage. Hitch fired twice. There was a spark on the garage's metal siding, but Kiddoni had again disappeared.

Kerra's heart did a somersault. Her Nephite warrior was *alive!*

Hitch shoved her, then Brock, toward the woods. *"Let's go! Move it!"*

They stumbled down into the ravine beyond the rusted Cadillac and entered the hollow.

•　•　•

Uncle Drew looked at his watch. It was almost evening. The shadows of the almond trees were long. His wife should have been here to pick him up. There were few things in Drew Whitman's life that he could count on since the accident that had injured his brain. One of them was the prompt arrival of Corinne at the end of his workday.

One of Drew's hired workers was in his truck, ready to drive away from the orchard. He called out the window, "Need a ride, Mr. Whitman?"

"Nah," said Drew. "That's all right. I believe I'll walk."

The worker studied him for a moment, then asked a little sheepishly, "Do you remember the way?"

Drew pulled in his chin in surprise. "To my house? Of course!"

"Okay," said the worker, still hesitant. Then he seemed to feel foolish and added, "Have a good night. See you tomorrow."

"All right," said Drew, feeling like he ought to call the worker by his name, though he couldn't possibly remember it.

The truck pulled away. Drew began walking home.

• • •

Grandpa Lee kept close to the back of the farmhouse, taking special care not to be seen through any windows. In his hands were Prince's AK-47 and Dushane's 12-gauge shotgun, both retrieved from the ground after Kiddoni had rendered the pair unconscious. He'd offered one to Kiddoni, but the Nephite had sternly refused, preferring his own armaments.

Gramdpa Lee noticed the old ladder lying horizontally along the base of the house, half hidden by weeds and spider webs. He looked up and saw that Skyler's second-story bedroom window was sitting partially open.

An idea began forming in the old man's mind.

• • •

Hitch, his finger still nervously set on the trigger of his 45-caliber handgun, followed Kerra and Brock into the midst of the broken slats and weathered fences of the old horse corral. Just ahead was a horse trough, its sides crimson with ancient rust. Brock glanced back at Hitch, then he climbed up inside the trough. Hitch licked his lips as the boy moved aside some brush and leaves, revealing the locked leather bag that Spree had given him on the night they left California.

The gangster reached out his hand. "It better all be there, kid. Or I'll lay you out like your friend, and I'll take great pleasure doing it."

Brock hesitated turning over the bag. His heart tightened into a knot as he realized what Hitch had said.

"You . . . you hurt Spree?" Brock asked.

Hitch chuckled and said sarcastically, "Yeah, that's right, kid. I 'hurt' him." He clenched his teeth. "Just hand it over."

Spree was seven years older than Brock, but he'd been the boy's best friend. *"He's just using you,"* his sister had warned many times, but Brock had always ignored her. Sure, he was no role model. But in his fatherless world, Brock wasn't choosy about alternatives. Anger and grief started boiling inside him.

Everyone's attention was suddenly drawn away as someone approached through the brush. Kerra's heart leaped. It was Kiddoni! The Nephite was poised with an arrow in his bow, string pulled back to his ear. Hitch reacted quickly. He turned to fire his pistol. But Kiddoni had already released the bowstring. Before Hitch could pull the trigger, the arrow struck his gun hand, piercing through the palm. The gangster let out a howl of pain and dropped his weapon into the weeds. With his good hand, he gripped onto the shaft of the arrow where it stabbed through his flesh.

Brock jumped out of the horse trough and dashed for the old stone well. Hitch saw where he was headed and, despite his agony, tried to cut him off. But the wounded gangster was too slow.

"*No!*" Hitch screamed.

It was too late. Brock had already hefted the leather bag filled with $250,000 worth of illegal drugs into the well. A hollow splash echoed up from the chamber below. Hitch, his eyes swelling with rage, glowered at the boy—the destroyer of his dreams, and probably his career—with the bitterest enmity. Kerra felt certain that he was about to use the bloodied arrowhead sticking out of his palm to actually stab downward on her brother. But then Hitch saw Kiddoni coming straight at him. He abandoned all hopes of revenge and fled into the trees.

Kerra rushed into Kiddoni's arms, embracing him tightly and failing to hold back her tears of relief. Kiddoni wanted to return the embrace, but he winced instead. The wound in his side was still quite tender.

Brock's mind immediately sprang back to his earlier emergency. "We have to go back there," he told his sister, pointing southward. "I met this guy. He saved my life. Kerra . . . he knows you."

Kerra's heart stopped. "*What?*" She released Kiddoni. "What did he look like?"

Brock replied impatiently, as if he would have preferred to give such details later. "Long beard and hair. They said he was a slave. But he saved me. Then he was attacked by these men—dozens of them. Their faces had black and white paint. But mostly they were smeared in blood."

"Giddianhi's army," declared Kiddoni.

"I think they're coming this way," Brock added.

Kiddoni turned sharply to Kerra. "The warning trumpet! Where is it?"

Kerra hardly heard the question. "This man might be my father," she said, her voice pleading.

She wanted desperately to follow Brock and find the man with the long beard. But Kiddoni grabbed her shoulders. She could see by his eyes that he felt such actions might be suicide. They had to deal first with the more immediate danger.

"There's no time to spare!" he shouted. "*The trumpet?*"

CHAPTER

14

ADDER WAS AS TAUT AS A TRIP WIRE, pacing like a caged tiger, checking all the windows, and then one minute later checking them again. His patience was at the breaking point. The youngest kid—Bernadette—was squalling to high heaven, and for all of the mother's efforts, she could not seem to get the brat to shut up. He was dangerously close to solving the problem for good. Adder feared that the kid's wailing would make unseen enemies more desperate to attack—speed up their rescue attempts. What if he just killed them all? One sweep of his AK would surely do the job. Who would ever know? In Adder's twisted mind this family had become a terrible burden—dead weight that he badly needed to cast off. The fact that they were alive endangered his very life, and for him to die in this fiasco was an unacceptable conclusion.

Corinne continued trying to calm Bernadette and the rest of her children. She could feel the gangster's mounting tension. His collar was ringed with sweat. His hands were shaking. She wouldn't have thought the situation could get any worse, but then Tessa started crying almost as loudly as Bernadette.

Adder pointed his weapon at Tessa's face. "Shut up!" He then pointed it at Corinne. "Shut them up, lady, or I swear—!"

Corinne was ready to break down, fall to her knees, and start pleading for mercy, but then her eyes turned toward the stairs. A noise had come from the second floor. Everybody stiffened in dread, especially Adder.

"Who's up there?" he asked Corinne, again threatening with his gun. "You hiding another kid?"

Corinne opened her mouth, but said nothing. Adder turned from her abruptly. Whatever had made that sound, it was going to die. There was no changing his mind. He was about to storm up the stairway, but then he hesitated. His primal, animal instincts had been alerted. If someone had infiltrated the second story of the house, Adder realized he might be rushing into a trap. He turned his head to see the fire pole in the corner of the living room. Cautiously he walked toward it, hoping it might give him a secret angle allowing him to spy on whoever might be hiding at the top of the stairs. His finger was on the trigger of his AK-47, ready to let loose a swarm of bullets.

As he drew closer, Adder did see something unusual. There *was* something up there, though he couldn't quite—

As Adder got in position beside the fire pole, his eyes widened in alarm. Something was falling!

Those were the gangster's last lucent thoughts before the wooden chest from Teancum's bedroom crashed on top of his head. He crumpled to the floor, dropping the weapon. Natasha, thinking quickly, leaped up from her chair and snatched up the gun from off the floor. Adder, despite his disorientation, tried to lunge at her.

Grandpa Lee's voice resonated at the top of the stairs. "I'd stop right there if I were you!"

Adder stopped abruptly, both hands raised above his

head. Corinne and the children turned to look at Grandpa Lee. He was coming down from the second floor, both hands filled with automatic weapons. The children's eyes bugged out in astonishment. Their grandfather looked like a septuagenarian Rambo.

• • •

Brock, Kerra, and Kiddoni arrived back at the clearing and began searching frantically for the ancient horn. Kiddoni was desperate to sound a warning to the other lookouts—lookouts who would in turn sound a warning to the entire Nephite army. Kerra was quickly becoming frustrated. Where could she have dropped it?

Her brother searched the area where Hitch had thrown Kerra onto the ground. Suddenly his hand reached down into the grass. "I found it!"

But just as Brock uttered these words, his eardrums rattled with the sound of a high, shrieking scream. As Brock turned, he saw the cleft-lipped Gadianton named Ogath charging toward them from the brush. Abruptly, Kiddoni pushed Brock aside, practically tossing him into the brambles. The Nephite drew out his saw-toothed sword. But before he could get the weapon into position, the assassin barreled into his chest. In a maneuver that seemed perfectly timed, Kiddoni dropped to the ground and flipped Ogath over his head and onto his back. The Gadianton tried to recover, but Kiddoni was too quick—too agile. He struck down with his sword's black stone spikes.

But just then another scream shook the clearing. Another assassin burst forth from the foliage on the opposite side. This time it was Shemish. In his arms was his seven-foot spear. He raised up the spear tip and swung it down hard toward the Nephite's head, like an ax blade. Kiddoni raised his own blade in the nick of time. Shemish's spear snapped in two. But the lithe assassin was not so easily defeated. He took the spear half with the tip and stabbed downward. Kiddoni rolled to the side. The point imbedded in the dirt. Thinking quickly, the Nephite grabbed the Gadianton's legs and tackled him. The two men began fighting viciously on the ground.

Brock watched the scene in stupefaction. It was like a dream—a dizzy, bewildering dream that left him almost feeling detached from mind and body. How could any of this be real? When he'd awakened that morning the world had been a normal place. Now he was watching men from an ancient century fighting hand to hand!

Suddenly Brock looked at the ancient horn in his hands, realizing what it was—what it meant. He started to put the instrument to his lips. Just then something smashed down violently on his wrist. The horn went flying again, this time flipping right into the fissure created by the earthquake. Brock's focus went blurry as the pain shot through his arm. He tumbled onto his side, tightly holding the injured limb. When his vision cleared, he saw Bakaan. The barrel-chested Gadianton had brought another spear down on Brock's hand, impacting just below the long stone point. Then he raised his spear back, its razor-sharp tip point aimed directly at Brock's chest. *He was finishing the job!*

"*Nooo!*" Kerra screamed.

She stood at the southern edge of the clearing, her face stretched in horror. The scream caused the big assassin to pause. Kiddoni's eyes also rose up. His knife had already made short work of Shemish. Like a Viking tossing an ax, Kiddoni hurled his sword at Bakaan. The weapon made one and a half circles as it approached its target, but Bakaan had seen it coming. He leaned back as the sawtooth points embedded in the tree behind his head. The smiling Gadianton now focused his attention squarely on the

Nephite, who was now armed only with his knife. The two men moved into the center of the clearing.

Kerra rushed to Brock, locking her arms around his chest. She started dragging him backwards, out of harm's way. Kiddoni and the Gadianton circled one another like wolves. Bakaan swung his spear a few times, testing the distance, but Kiddoni dodged it, leaping back.

"The horn!" Kerra said to Brock anxiously. "Where did it land?"

The boy, still wincing in pain, pointed toward the fissure with his uninjured hand. Kerra rushed over to the area, frantically searching the weeds all around.

The big Gadianton made another shriek for momentum as he thrust the spear straight at Kiddoni's chest. Kiddoni twisted hard, raising his arm. The spear missed his chest, but as it bit into the trunk of the fallen cottonwood, it ripped a tear in his shoulder armor. Kiddoni burst forward, throwing Bakaan into the briars. He tried to stab at Bakaan with his knife, but the assassin caught his arm.

Kerra saw it! The horn was in the crevasse! It was balanced precariously in the gap about three feet down. Beneath it, the crevasse seemed to widen. One false move and the horn would drop hopelessly out of reach. Kerra lay against the ground along the edge of the fissure.

Kiddoni and Bakaan continued to grapple. The Gadianton held Kiddoni's knife arm at bay as he reached with his other hand and grasped a thorny thistle, crushing it into Kiddoni's face. As the Nephite turned his face away, Bakaan seized Kiddoni's knife arm with both hands. He began pounding Kiddoni's wrist against the stones, rabid to knock the weapon free. As it fell, the Gadianton lunged for it. In turn, Kiddoni lunged for the spear point that had been imbedded in the cottonwood. As Bakaan came at him for the kill, Kiddoni yanked the spear free and rolled onto his back, directing the point upward.

A cry of agony wrenched out of the big Gadianton's throat. He went limp and dropped to his knees. Kiddoni pulled the spear back, letting the assassin fall to the side.

Kerra was still reaching into the crevasse. "Kiddoni!" she shouted.

The Nephite heaved for oxygen. Kerra's voice jarred him back to reality. Unsteadily, he got back to his feet. Kerra's arm and shoulder were reaching in as far as she could.

"The horn!" Kerra continued. "I can't quite reach it! I need your arm!"

Kiddoni nodded, still slightly disoriented, and took a step toward her. But then his back arched. The warrior's shoulder twisted forward as an arrow pierced his flesh, spinning him around. Kiddoni dropped to the ground, writhing. Behind him, at the edge of the brush, stood the final assassin. Brock recognized Lord Kush immediately.

Her veins boiling with desperation, Kerra strained again to reach the horn. Calmly, the leader of the assassins stepped out of the brush, into the clearing, and pulled a second arrow from his quiver.

She could touch it! But she couldn't find a grip! At best, she felt she would only knock it out of place and lose it forever! The Gadianton loaded his bow, aiming it directly at Kerra's head. He drew the string back toward his eye.

The wind was knocked from Kush's lungs as Brock launched into his stomach. The boy's weight was hardly enough to send the Gadianton off balance, but as the bowstring snapped, the arrow's nock became tangled—no missile was launched! Kush grabbed Brock by the scruff of the neck and tossed him off as easily as a yipping puppy. Then he leaned down to pick up the arrow.

Kerra strained one last time with all her might, the rocky edge of the fissure grinding into her shoulder blade and neck. *She grasped it!* Her fingers hoisted Kiddoni's horn out of the fissure. Kush was just setting the arrow back onto the string as

Kerra pulled herself up. She blew into the instrument with all the power in her lungs. The woods were filled with a bellowing echo, like the blast of a trumpet, but more deep-pitched, and with a vibration to shake the foundations of the earth.

Kush gritted his teeth in fury. He lifted the bow to fire just as Kerra released a second blast on the horn, even louder than the first. The tip was already aimed, the string pulling back, as the hills echoed with a resounding reply—another horn, from another ridge.

The leader of the assassins stopped cold. It was too late. *Too late!* The alarm had been sounded. Kerra remained there on her knees, looking straight down the shaft of the Gadianton's arrow. In his eyes Kerra perceived a pale dread, as if her actions had sealed this man's fate. Kush glanced around at his fallen comrades, then paid Kerra one last scathing look. His fingers finished pulling back the bow-string. But as he brought the nock to his eye, he suddenly straightened as stiff as a fence post, eyes popping wide.

In disbelief, Kerra watched him fall forward, dead. There was an arrow piercing right between the shoulder blades of his back.

She blinked her eyes. There was someone else beyond him in the forest. In that person's hands was an empty bow. Kerra squinted to see who it was, but the setting sun was right behind his head. She could tell that he had a long beard, but his other features were indistinct. Certainly it was this man's arrow that had killed the Gadianton.

The figure stepped toward her, and immediately his face came out of the brightness. Kerra looked into his eyes. He was dressed in an ancient mantle; his face was bruised and scratched—but those *eyes!* Kerra's mind tumbled back a hundred years—a thousand years—to the faraway glimpses of her early childhood, when memories were more like dreams, and images were fogged around the edges. Yet despite the passage of time, and despite the multitude of other memories piled on top of it, *this* image was as sharp today as when she was five years old. It was as vivid as the day she'd watched him walk out the front door with a hunting rifle in his arms.

"Sakerra?" uttered Chris softly, still approaching.

Kerra nodded, her eyes filling with tears.

"Daddy," she responded, because that was the only word she knew for him. The only name she'd ever used.

Chris McConnell filled his arms with his daughter, embracing her with all the joy in his weary heart. Brock came forward as well, now looking at the bearded man in an entirely new light. Chris reached out toward his son. Brock hesitantly held out his uninjured hand for him to take, then was drawn into the embrace. All three of them could feel the sacred warmth: the embrace of a family reunited.

The echo of more warning trumpets resounded in the distance, some near, some far.

• • •

Uncle Drew had just walked past his father-in-law's violin shop and was starting down the long driveway to his house when he paused abruptly. From here he could overlook much of the hollow from the east, and in the distance he could hear the cacophony of ancient trumpets.

• • •

Young Tessa leaned against the counter, looking through the dining room window that faced the hollow to the south. The sun was setting fast, and the harsh contrast of shadows caused her to squint her eyes. Yet she was sure that she could see people—dozens of them—coming from the woods and heading toward the farmhouse.

She turned to her mother and asked innocently, "Mommy, who are those men?"

Corinne and Grandpa Lee came into the kitchen to see what she was pointing at. When Corinne saw it, she gasped to the pit of her stomach. It was a line of Gadianton warriors, caked in blood and armed to the teeth with spears, swords, bows, and other ancient weapons. To Corinne and Grandpa Lee it seemed as if the warriors *coalesced* from the woods, almost like ghosts emerging from another dimension and entering the modern realm.

As Adder realized that his subjugators were thoroughly distracted, he made a break for it, rushing out the front door. Grandpa saw him flee, but he was too stunned by what he saw through the window to care.

"It's the invasion," he whispered to Corinne.

"*What?*" asked Corinne, beside herself in disbelief.

Grandpa Lee wasn't about to take the time to explain. "We have to get out of here—*now!*"

As Adder leaped from the front porch, he saw Prince and Dushane groggily coming to their feet. Adder turned around once and took in the same vision as Corinne and Grandpa Lee. There were hundreds of Gadiantons now, stalking closer. The first of them had nearly reached the southern edge of the Whitmans' yard.

"*Keys!*" Adder cried, rushing up to his comrades. "*Who has the keys?*"

Prince, still disoriented, focused his vision on the approaching warriors. He shut his eyes tightly, then opened them again with a shake of his head. "What in the—?"

"Just drive the car!" Adder threw open the rear door of the Acura NSX-T and practically dove into the back seat. Prince pulled the keys from his pocket and jumped behind the steering wheel. He started the engine and threw it into gear.

"Wait!" cried Dushane. Since his comrades wouldn't slow down to allow him to open the door, he settled for diving through the open passenger's side window. His feet were still dangling out as Prince punched the gas and sped up the driveway.

The Acura zipped past Uncle Drew, who had reached the bottom of the hill. He continued running toward his house. Five seconds later, the gangsters also drove past Hitch, though they didn't see him. Their illustrious leader was still standing within the trees, trembling in pain as he broke the shaft of Kiddoni's arrow and yanked it out of his hand. As Hitch saw his sports car fast approaching, he scrambled to reach the road.

"HEYYY!"

But the Acura screamed on by. Hitch ran out into the middle of the driveway, still frenetically waving his uninjured arm and howling in frustration, but his sports car was soon up the hill and out of sight.

Uncle Drew reached the front porch just as his family was coming out of the house. The Gadianton warriors were less than twenty-five yards away now, and still closing in. Grandpa Lee was carrying Sariah and pulling Tessa by the elbow. Aunt Corinne saw her husband and embraced his shoulders.

"Drew, we have to leave!"

"I know!" said Drew, sounding surprisingly lucent—more aware and cognizant than he'd sounded in over a decade. "*Everyone!* In the van! Go! Go!"

Corinne turned back, counting her children in a single glance. "Bernadette? WHERE'S BERNADETTE!" She looked at Natasha, who she'd thought was carrying the toddler, but Natasha shook her head, eyes full of fright.

"I'll get her!" announced Grandpa Lee.

He handed off Sariah to Drew, then darted back inside the house, searching anxiously. He spotted the AK-47s that he'd set down on the counter in order to carry Sariah. If he was going to continue searching, he decided he might need one of those guns. But just as he moved to retrieve it, the glass shattered on the window of the side door. A hand—dyed a deep red—reached through the broken pane, fumbling with the latch, as if uncertain how this contraption called a door was supposed to work. At last the warrior figured it out and stepped into the kitchen, blocking the way from the dining room. Behind him entered another Gadianton, also adorned in leather and animal claws, also dyed in blood. Both men wore helmets in the shape of jaguar skulls, the fangs coming under their chins and around their faces. They stood mesmerized by all the unfamiliar trappings, testing the air with their spears, as if the two weapons were insect antennae.

Grandpa Lee stood as still as a statue, as if he actually hoped the warriors might not notice him, despite the fact that he stood squarely in the center of the living room. At that instant he saw little Bernadette step out from behind the kitchen counter, just three feet from the warrior-demons. In her hands was an empty sipper cup. The Gadiantons gaped down at her. Eyes full of innocence, she held the cup toward them.

"Juice? More juice?"

Grandpa Lee came forward. He smiled at the two men and nodded, as if bidding them a friendly hello. The men looked so stunned by his actions that they just stood there, watching.

Suddenly Grandpa Lee scooped up the two-year-old and made a mad dash toward the front door. More warriors entered the side door. One of them—obviously a commander—chastised his men for standing there like tree trunks. He ordered them to take up pursuit. The Gadiantons rushed after Grandpa Lee and Bernadette, swords raised and ready to strike.

●   ●   ●

Kiddoni gritted his teeth in pain as Kerra and Chris helped him to stand. He used the trunk of an old black willow tree for support. Brock stood close by, still massaging his injured wrist. The arrow remained imbedded in Kiddoni's shoulder.

Brock, still mesmerized by the sight of this man whom Kerra had called her father, asked him, "How did you get away?"

"Long story," Chris replied. "Suffice it to say, if you capture someone, don't stand around arguing about who gets to slay him. Your captive just might spot an opportunity and take it. Might even steal a weapon." He nodded toward the bow he'd used moments before, now leaning against the tree.

At last, Kiddoni managed to stand on his own. Kerra tried to wrap her arms around his waist to offer further support, but Kiddoni rejected it.

"No, I'm all right. I'm all right now."

Brock suddenly turned toward the woods to the south. "They're coming!"

The forest was alive with sounds—hundreds of bodies moving through the brush. Kiddoni interpreted the sounds immediately.

"It's Giddianhi's army. Go, all of you! Seek shelter! Hide!"

"But we can't leave you," said Kerra. "You're wounded!"

"I can still run! Our army—Captain Gidgiddoni—will be coming too. *You have to get out of here!*"

He looked at Chris, who he seemed certain would understand the urgency. Brock also looked anxious to leave. But Kerra lingered, holding Kiddoni's hand, fear and doubt clouding her eyes. A tear dropped on her cheek as she managed to choke out, "I'll see you again." It was a statement, not a question—as if she were issuing a command.

"Yes," he said adamantly. But then his confidence seemed to falter for an instant, and he added more poetically, "Every sunrise and sunset."

Kerra wanted certainty, not poetry, but Chris took his daughter's shoulders. "Sakerra, we have to go."

The shadows of the Gadianton warriors were visible now through the trees.

"*RUN!*" Kiddoni shouted at them.

Reluctantly, Kerra released Kiddoni's hand and took her father's instead. Brock also held onto Chris, and the three of them leaped across the fissure, entering the thick foliage.

Kiddoni stood and watched them a moment, bracing his injured shoulder with his other arm. The distant trumpets sounded again, almost like a fanfare. Kiddoni staggered toward the sound, disappearing into the trees to the north.

• • •

Uncle Drew took Bernadette from Grandpa Lee's arms as the old man came across the driveway. Aunt Corinne was already behind the wheel, struggling to fit the key into the ignition. Everyone reached for the van doors and flung themselves inside as dozens of Gadianton warriors approached. Warriors wearing helmets made from skulls emerged from behind the garage. They marched around both sides of the trampoline. They poured out the front door of the house, rapidly surrounding the van. Skyler quickly pulled the van's side door shut. The children clung to one another in the backseats as Corinne finally turned the key in the ignition. But the engine wouldn't turn over. As she leaned back, she saw a Gadianton standing at her car window, glaring in. The whites of his eyes stood out like glistening porcelain. He watched Corinne's actions with intense curiosity, trying to figure out what she was doing. Corinne continued to struggle with the ignition, muttering a string of Mormon-ized curse words.

"Fetch! Shoot! Come on! COME ON!"

At last the engine fired and roared. But before she could throw it into gear, the Gadianton smashed the blunt end of his spear toward Corinne's head. The driver's side window transformed into a spiderweb of cracks. Children shrieked and screamed. Corinne punched the gas. The car lurched forward, sending the Gadiantons on all sides of the vehicle scurrying out of the way. Spears were hurled, the stone tips impacting the sides of the van and leaving hefty dents in the rear door. A few warriors chased them down the driveway, but the Maxiwagon van safely sped out of their grasp.

• • •

Chris, Kerra, and Brock tore through the undergrowth, illuminated now only by twilight. The woods had turned into a raucous pandemonium of marching men calling to each other, raising war cries. Kerra realized the echo of the Whistlers was more penetrating than ever, seeping into the marrow of her soul. As they arrived at the old horse corral, Chris spotted a withered shed, partially leaning over on its side, and nearly suffocated by weeds and brush. He yanked at the wooden door, almost pulling it off its rusted hinges.

"In here!" he said sternly.

The three of them slipped inside and hunkered down in the cramped space, stale with the smell of dust and festooned with cobwebs. Through the slats between the panels of weathered wood they began to perceive hundreds of silhouettes. Gadianton warriors were pouring through the area, their pace quickening as their march worked its way northward. Chris held his children tightly, determined with all his heart to keep them safe. It was a fatherly instinct—and privilege—that he had never experienced with his two children from the modern world.

• • •

Hitch Ventura fought his way through the woods, holding his bleeding hand and frequently checking his back. He could see the mysterious warriors in the forest behind him, ever drawing closer. Hitch swallowed hard. Looking straight ahead, he saw an archway created by twisting limbs and aimed directly for it.

As he passed underneath the arch, Hitch abruptly drew to a halt, eyes as wide as stop signs. The scene had *changed!* He was standing in a *jungle!* Yet the sky was still bright orange with the colors of the sunset. Hitch let out a terrified yelp and lurched backwards.

The scene changed again. He was back in the hollow. Hitch twisted around. The ancient warriors were emerging from the trees. *They were coming right at him!*

Again he jumped underneath the arch. Sure enough, he was again surrounded by a lush green jungle. But when he looked back, to his horror, the warriors with their spears and axes were still marching straight at him—and at exactly the same distance! The setting was different, but the positioning of the ghosts, or Indians, or whatever they were, was exactly the same. Hitch crashed through a nest of jungle ferns. The shadows were thick—he couldn't see where he was going— yet he continued to run.

The ground dropped out from beneath his feet. Hitch tumbled into a gully, shrieking in pain as he twice rolled over his injured hand. As he recovered and looked about, he saw some rocks to his left. He spotted a cavity where he might hide. Hitch slipped hastily inside, all the while mutter- ing Hail Marys and several other prayers that he hadn't uttered since he was six years old.

• • •

Part of the shed's roof was missing, allowing Kerra to look up at the stars—just now twinkling into view. She could also see the last purple ribbon of the setting sun that outlined the hills to the northwest.

Her father raised his eyes as they heard the echo of

another trumpet, sounding much like the horn that had belonged to Kiddoni. Then they heard another trumpet—closer. In the hazy distance, Kerra swore that she could hear the clatter of swords and shields and the cries of men as they clashed on the field of battle. She pressed deeper into her father's arms. But then she turned her face away, fresh tears filling her eyes as she thought of Kiddoni. Had her Nephite warrior managed to outrun the enemy phalanx? How could he survive with an arrow in his shoulder?

"He's out there in that," she whispered to her father. "Kiddoni is out there."

"I know," he replied. "It'll be all right. I promise."

To her surprise, his words brought her surprising comfort. Chris hugged his two children more tightly as shadows continued rushing past their hiding place, none stopping or slowing down. In time the darkness became too thick for them to make out the warriors' shapes, but they continued to hear intermittent footsteps, some running forward, some even running back. And in the distance, the echoes of ancient warfare continued to reverberate throughout the night.

CHAPTER

15

CHRIS AND BROCK WERE ASLEEP, leaning against one another at the rear of the shed. Kerra had shut her eyes, barely dozing, her mind filled with trumpets and voices, although it was hard to tell how many of them had emanated from the distant battles and how many were created by her dreams. The first vague glimmer of sunrise had begun to appear in the sky, gently pushing away the night. Kerra opened her eyes once to see it, but the image didn't really register in her consciousness. Her thoughts drifted off to other vistas.

The three of them continued to doze as the sounds in the hollow became ever more calm and quiet. Then something else stirred deep within the earth. It was first revealed as the old, weathered wood of the shed began to creak. As Kerra felt the rumbling, her eyes flew open. The tremor lasted only two or three more seconds, like the restless soul of a mountain turning over in its sleep. Then it stopped. Nothing more.

The sleepy voice of her father uttered something in the darkness. The word seemed so alien, so otherworldly, that Kerra took a second to grasp its meaning. Then it became clear.

"Aftershock," he had said.

177

Kerra sat forward, her mind as wide awake as at noon-day, adrenaline coursing through her veins. It struck her why her father's voice had sounded so alien. There was nothing in the background to accompany it. No hum. No whispering.

The Whistlers had gone silent.

Kerra gasped as if she were being strangled. The sound brought Chris and her brother to full alertness.

"What is it?" asked Brock.

Kerra came to her feet and rushed out of the shed. She stood in the open, listening hard. Brock and her father joined her, watching her actions with intense curiosity. A moment later Chris also seemed to realize the woods were different. Everything was much too quiet.

"It's gone," said Kerra.

"What?" asked Brock.

"The Whistlers! *They're gone!*"

Brock looked perplexed, apparently not understanding what would be so upsetting about the disappearance of a sound. The boy turned suddenly as he saw something in the woods behind them. It was a flashlight beam, cutting through the thick shadows of twilight. A figure came forth from the brush. It was Grandpa Lee.

He called to them. "Kerra! Brock!"

At a distance of about ten yards, Grandpa Lee stopped in surprise. He shone his light directly in Chris's face—into the face of his son. He moved away the light, as if only the nat-ural light of morning could completely tell the truth. Grandpa Lee was speechless.

The emotion heavy in his voice, Chris spoke first. "Hello, Dad."

At last Grandpa Lee spoke his son's name, though it was barely a whisper. "Chris!"

He came forward. Son and father embraced. Grandpa Lee began weeping unashamedly. But just then Kerra broke into a run and disappeared into the woods.

"Kerra!" Brock called after her.

Kerra didn't falter. She tore through the undergrowth and finally broke through the last barrier of black willow trees. Her legs crossed over the fissure, and she burst into the clearing, turning every which way, her eyes searching the area in desperation.

They were gone!—the bodies of the Gadianton assassins, the arrows and other abandoned and broken weapons. *Gone!* Someone had taken them all away!

No, it was worse. It was as if they'd *never been here!* There seemed to be no evidence whatsoever of any disturbance in the area. Then her fingers grasped out at the trunk of the cottonwood where she'd seen Kiddoni grappling with one of the Gadiantons. She felt the place where she was sure that one of their spears had struck. It was still there!—the notch. The broken spear was nowhere to be seen. But the *notch* was there—the chip in the bark.

Yet it meant nothing. Only that she wasn't insane. Just that everything had happened as she'd remembered it. But why were there no bodies? Why no weapons? Why had the ambient humming sound of the hollow disappeared?

Grandpa Lee's flashlight flickered from the trees as he, Chris, and Brock entered the clearing and found Kerra on the ground, her back against the stone. The girl looked utterly broken and distraught. The light of dawn had increased slightly, so Grandpa Lee switched off his light. As they approached Kerra, she was weeping, shaking her head.

Without looking up, she declared, "It's gone. The rift is gone."

• • •

Uncle Drew entered the house to find his wife standing in the living room. The place was in shambles. Tables and chairs had been overturned. Couches and couch cushions were displaced and flung about. The television and everything else in the entertainment center had been knocked down and strewn from one end of the house to the other. The trail of debris led through the front door and actually continued several hundred feet up the driveway. It looked as if an army had marched through their living room. And indeed, one had.

But as Uncle Drew crossed the room to comfort his wife, he noticed something at his feet and leaned down to pick it up. Corinne, watching his actions, came over to see what he'd found. Drew lifted up a family portrait. It was face down, but as he turned it over, they both saw that it was perfectly intact. The frame was unbent, the glass unbroken.

"Hey," he said to Corinne. "Look. Nothing broken. Nothing lost."

Corinne looked into her husband's eyes. She wasn't sure if he even remembered what had happened the previous night, and it really didn't matter. He couldn't have expressed it any better. Their children were all outside in the van, some sleeping, others waiting for an all-clear sign from their parents. But all of them were safe and well.

She embraced her husband in the midst of the wreckage. "Yes," she replied. "Nothing lost."

• • •

Hitch Ventura emerged from the cavity in the rocks. He'd hoped to discover that he was waking up from a bizarre nightmare—some kind of flashback invoked by bad drugs. But the green and lush world that he'd entered the previous night was all around him, now illuminated by the soft light of morning. Apparently the nightmare wasn't over.

His arm was now tied up in a sling that he'd made from his torn shirt, exposing the dragon tattoo on his shoulder that designated him as a Shaman. Strewn about the ground were the bodies of several of the blood-painted warriors who had come after him the previous night, obviously killed in all the fighting that he'd heard throughout the darkness. But killed by whom?

Hitch turned with a start as he heard someone coming. From the jungle about twenty yards to the left appeared several dozen men. But they weren't dressed like the men on the ground. No blood-smeared faces. No skull helmets. Still, their clothing was like something out of a Tarzan movie. Or was it like out of a gladiator movie? Not that he was going to stick around and ask. Several were raising up their weapons threateningly.

Hitch bolted into the foliage. He scrambled up the ravine that he'd fallen down the previous night. Soon he reached the place where he'd "crossed over" into the jungle world. But as he tried to run back across the barrier—as he tried to return home—nothing happened. There was no change of scenery. In fact, the battalion of approaching warriors thought he looked rather ridiculous jumping back and forth like a lunatic.

"*What's wrong?*" Hitch exclaimed out loud. "*What's going on?*"

Finally, as Hitch realized that he was surrounded, he stopped jumping and faced the ancient warriors, a look of defiance on his face. That is, defiance mingled with old-fashioned, gut-twisting fear.

"Captain Gidgiddoni," one of the men called back.

A large man came forward through the ranks, clearly some kind of commander, by the look of his uniform and decorated helmet. The man stopped about five feet away. He looked at Hitch's face, then at the dragon tattoo on Hitch's arm. The Nephite commander thinned his eyes menacingly. He pointed at the tattoo and pronounced his verdict to the men:

"Gadianton."

●　●　●

Kerra sat on the stone in the center of the clearing. She felt as if her heart had been torn down the middle. Her father, Brock, and Grandpa Lee remained nearby as she stared at that place in the trees where she'd once seen Kiddoni coalesce from the nothingness and walk over to join her. She felt helpless, and even a little ungrateful. The rift had brought back her father. But not Kiddoni. Still, she continued to hope, continued to stare. If only, thought Kerra, the power of the rift could be influenced by sheer desire. By wanting something badly enough. By love. She scoffed at herself. Ridiculous. Only another earthquake, flood, or some other phenomenon could restore the miracle. And that might not happen for years. Another millennium. Or never.

At last her father laid a hand on her shoulder. "Come on, honey," he said solemnly.

Kerra looked up at him, smiling, though her eyes remained moist. She heaved a deep sigh. The sigh was laced with sadness, but also with satisfaction. She covered her father's hand with her own and started to stand. She sent Brock and Grandpa Lee the same loving smile, and then she walked to the edge of the clearing. After turning once to pay the place a final farewell glance, she faced the trail leading home. But before stepping across the fissure, her foot stopped, almost in midair.

She'd heard something. Very faint. Almost *too* faint. So quiet that after a few seconds she decided her ears must have been mistaken. The others apparently hadn't heard it. They were looking at her strangely, wondering why she'd paused. But then, as she again faced the clearing, she heard it a second time.

"Sakerra."

Her heart skipped a beat. The lump in her throat swelled. The voice was foggy and full of echoes, but there was no mistaking its owner. It was Kiddoni. She looked around in a panic. There was no one there. No blurry image, no hazy mirage. There was nothing out of the ordinary among the stark morning shadows. And yet she was *sure* . . .

"Is something wrong?" asked Brock.

"Shh!" said Grandpa Lee.

So she wasn't the only one who'd heard it. Kerra thought back to that very first instance when she and Kiddoni had come face-to-face in the midst of the thistle patch. She'd taken a step across the fissure and *wham!*—he'd appeared out of nowhere. They had nearly collided. It occurred to her that this rift could be very particular about its location—very specific, even down to the precise square yard or foot. The others watched curiously as she wandered around the edges of the clearing, turning in circles, as if she were literally trying to spook up a ghost. Her eyes focused everywhere, fully expecting an image to coalesce from the empty space. He was here. She *felt* it! But *where?*

She walked to the other end of the clearing, past the rock. That was where she caught her first glimpse. He was standing just beyond the log that lay across the ground, but she took one step too far. When she finally halted, he was gone again. Kerra backtracked—*very, very* slowly. And two seconds later, his image materialized again, like a flash of glare on a mirror.

He was smiling at her—so boldly and lovingly that Kerra's heart turned to water. He no longer wore his heavy armor—just a simple tunic and belt. No helmet—just his trusty, sawtoothed sword behind his shoulder. In fact, his shoulder was bound up in bandages from the wound inflicted by the Gadianton's arrow. There were no signs of further injury. Just that bright, glorious smile, like a man utterly certain of what he felt in his mind and heart.

The others couldn't tell what Kerra was looking at. Brock started to come forward, determined to see what Kerra was seeing, but his father and Grandpa Lee stopped him. They knew Kiddoni must be there, and they wisely believed that no one should interfere. Such interference might disturb the rift. Besides, this was Kerra's moment. A moment for her and Kiddoni alone.

She reached out reflexively, wanting to touch him, hold him. But as his image shimmered, she realized that the rift was more fragile than ever. There was nothing to touch, nothing to hold. Kerra felt an aching disappointment. Yet she stood up tall and sent him back the same loving smile.

"I see you're all right."

"Yes," he replied, his voice foggy and echoing. "The battle was won. The Gadiantons have been driven back. Their leader, Giddianhi, is slain. The Gadianton forces are seriously depleted, as well as their ability to ever be a serious threat to us again. And it's because of you, Sakerra."

Kerra shook her head. "No. It was *you*. You were right all along. They came right through here, just as you always knew they would."

He suddenly looked concerned. "Your father and brother?"

"They're all right," said Kerra. "They're here. They're behind me. Can't you . . . can't you see them?"

Kiddoni shook his head. "No. I see only you. So faint."

Sadly, Kerra said, "The rift is fading."

"I know," said Kiddoni. "But not forever. It won't fade away forever." He paused, wanting to express his next words carefully. "You taught me something . . . something besides hate. I wanted to . . . thank you. I love you, Sakerra."

Tears pricked at Kerra's eyes, and she replied painfully, "I love you too."

"It was so long before," said Kiddoni, sighing. "I waited so long. Please . . . don't make me wait so long again."

"No," said Kerra. "Not so long. I'll see you again. I believe it. I know it. I'll never forget you, Kiddoni."

She brought her hand forward, not expecting to touch anything. But his hand came forward as well, and as their molecules intermingled, she *did* feel something. More than warmth, and definitely not pain. She was certain that somehow their hands supported each other's weight. Kerra shut her eyes, and for a second the sensation was no different than if her hand had been placed directly inside his powerful grip. In fact, the sensation was *better.* As if a part of them seemed literally like one.

Kiddoni leaned forward. Carefully, lightly, he set his lips on hers. Although her eyes remained shut, she swore she could feel his kiss, warm and perfect.

Afterwards, he drew back a little and whispered, "Goodbye, Sakerra. My little angel."

As Kerra opened her eyes, his image flickered again. It seemed to have faded markedly. She did not want to see him disappear. She wasn't sure she could stand it. So she backed away, just a few inches, and sent him another glowing smile.

Unlike Kerra, Kiddoni was determined not to miss a single instant. As long as she was visible, he wasn't going to move a single step. But Kerra slowly turned around, lingering another moment, tempted to face him again. Then her lungs filled with air and she walked back toward her father, brother, and grandfather.

Only as she reached the edge of the clearing did she turn back. As expected, the Nephite was gone. She'd known that he would be. She'd turned only so she could remember the place, memorize the exact spot, so that when she returned here, she would know it at once.

Her father put his arm around her shoulders and embraced her. At last the family turned away from the clearing and made their way back through the brush toward the farmhouse. Brock reached out and took his sister's hand. Kerra squeezed his hand back with all the love in her heart.

Then she closed her eyes and concentrated, already listening again for the sweet, faint song of the Whistlers.

ABOUT THE AUTHOR

Chris Heimerdinger currently lives in Riverton, Utah with his wife, Beth, and his four children, Steven, Ammon, Alyssa, and Liahona. He has written more than fifteen novels in several different genres, but all of them with the unmistakable stamp of high adventure.

He began writing at the age of seven, completing his very first book at the age of eight—an adventure entitled *Howl of the Wolf Pack,* with wolf cubs as his main characters. This was followed up two years later with a science fiction entitled *The Reptiles,* wherein Chris featured himself as the main character, finding a prehistoric egg, hatching his own pet dinosaur, and eventually raising up an army of dinosaurs to take over the world.

Since then Chris' ambitions have changed very little. He *still* wants to take over the world, but instead of using dinosaurs, he strives to utilize the pure gospel of Jesus Christ.

The story for *Passage to Zarahemla* was first hatched in 1999 under the title "Summer of the Nephite," then honed and refined for four years to its current form. Chris explains, "I always saw this as a movie, first and foremost. I've never written a story based so heavily on a very specific location. The wooded hollow in southern Utah, the McConnell's farmhouse, even the violin shop, are actual locations that will be used for filming." Chris hopes to begin shooting the principle scenes of *Passage to Zarahemla* in the spring of 2004, with an anticipated release 6–12 months later.

In the near future Chris also hopes to release a sequel to his beloved 1993 novel *Eddie Fantastic,* along with an updated and revised version of the original. He will also release *Muckwhip's Guide to Capturing the Latter-day Soul*— a witty satire along the same lines as C.S. Lewis' *Screwtape Letters*—and, of course, the tenth installment of his celebrated "Tennis Shoes Adventure Series."

Soon Chris also plans to release a narrated edition of the Book of Mormon, performed with the same dynamics and passion as the audio versions of all his novels.

To learn more about Chris and his upcoming projects, including the movie, *Passage to Zarahemla,* visit his website and become a registered guest at *www. cheimerdinger.com.*